TO CATCH HIS MATE

A CRESCENT MOON STORY

Savannah Stuart

Copyright © 2015 by Savannah Stuart

All rights reserved. Except as permitted under the U.S. Copyright Act of 1976, no part of this publication may be reproduced, distributed, or transmitted in any form or by any means, or stored in a database or retrieval system, without the prior written permission of the author. Thank you for buying an authorized version of this book and complying with copyright laws. You're supporting writers and encouraging creativity.

Cover art: Jaycee of Sweet 'N Spicy Designs
Author website: www.savannahstuartauthor.com

Publisher's Note: This is a work of fiction. Names, characters, places, and incidents are either the products of the author's imagination or used fictitiously, and any resemblance to actual persons, living or dead, or business establishments, organizations or locales is completely coincidental.

To Catch His Mate/KR Press, LLC -- 1st ed.

ISBN-10: 1942447388
ISBN-13: 9781942447382

eISBN: 9781942447375

Praise for the books of Savannah Stuart

"Fans of sexy paranormal romance should definitely treat themselves to this sexy & fun story." —Nina's Literary Escape

"I enjoyed this installment so much I'll be picking up book one...worth the price for the punch of plot and heat."
—Jessie, HEA USA Today blog

"...a scorching hot read." —The Jeep Diva

"This story was a fantastic summer read!" —Book Lovin' Mamas

"If you're looking for a hot, sweet read, be sure not to miss Tempting Alibi. It's one I know I'll revisit again and again."
—Happily Ever After Reviews

"You will not regret reading the previous story or this one. I would recommend it to anyone who loves a great shifter story."
—The Long & Short of It

"...a fun and sexy shapeshifter book and definitely worth the read."
—The Book Binge

PROLOGUE

Alyssa didn't bother knocking as she opened the front door to Reece's house. As alpha of the O'Shea pack he was used to a lot of foot traffic and since she was here as his guest—and intended mate—he'd told her that she had full reign over his place.

That still felt a little weird, but tonight she'd decided to take him up on it. At first she'd been pissed at her father for setting up this whole 'arranged mating'. It was so archaic. But then she'd met Reece and thought maybe they had a chance at happiness... maybe more.

She'd grown up sheltered, that being the understatement of the century, but she'd dated in college. Sort of. Usually her dates had been shadowed by one of her packmates, per her father's orders. Still, she'd gone out with males before and the physical attraction she felt toward Reece was a hundred on the Richter scale compared to what she'd felt for other males.

Her feet were silent as she hurried up the stairs. She'd tried out a new cloaking scent one of her packmates had given her that was supposed to cover her natural scent. It was a body lotion that smelled like, well, nothing. It was the first time she'd tried anything like it and she wanted to see if it worked. And if she could surprise an alpha then it was definitely the real deal.

That wasn't her only reason for coming to see him. She really wanted to kiss Reece again—and she had a gift for him. He'd mentioned that he loved a certain baseball team so she'd gotten him a vintage ball cap. It had taken some searching, but she'd found one online and had paid for the faster shipping so it would get here in time.

She hoped that tonight led to more than just kissing too. Reece had been so restrained the past few weeks. Always pulling back after heated kisses when she could tell that he physically wanted more. Her experience with the opposite sex might be limited, but she'd felt his erections against her stomach and as a wolf shifter she had a heightened sense of smell and scented his desire. Some things a male simply couldn't hide.

But she'd started to wonder if maybe that wasn't enough for him. God, what did she really know about males? Maybe he didn't want this mating because... whatever reason. There were tons she could think of. His pack was smaller and he was a young alpha at only thirty-five so their mating was supposed to strengthen both their packs on the South Carolina coast.

Tonight she wanted to find out if there could be more between them than just some hot kisses. She already really liked him and not just in the physical sense. He was a good alpha, he'd been incredibly sweet to her since she'd arrived, bringing her over coffee and pastries every morning, and talking to her as if she mattered—unlike some alphas she'd interacted with. He was a little intense sometimes and she'd found she loved making him laugh or smile. She'd noticed he rarely seemed to smile except around her.

Pretty much his entire pack was at some Halloween festival at their local downtown but she knew he had paperwork to catch up on.

So she was hoping to catch *him*.

As she reached the top of the stairs she heard low murmured voices. Both male. One was definitely Reece. She got shivers just hearing the low rumble. Everything about the male seemed to affect her.

When she heard another familiar voice, she paused. Ugh, Reece was talking to Ben. For some reason the other male didn't seem to like her and Alyssa couldn't figure out why. She'd become friends with his sister, Sybil, the past few weeks and she couldn't think of anything she'd done to warrant his coldness toward her. But the male just looked at her with annoyance.

Reece might have told her she had free reign here but that didn't mean she wanted to see or talk to Ben. She started to head back down the stairs but froze at a growling sound.

Not Reece, but Ben.

On instinct her claws started to ache, ready to be unleashed, but her inner wolf stilled when Ben spoke. "Damn it! Why are you mating with her?"

"You know why." Reece's voice was calm but there was a deadly edge to his words that made it clear who was in charge. She was actually surprised that Ben had the balls to even talk to Reece like that.

"We don't need the strength of her pack. We've been doing fine, more than fine, on our own for years. We're strong enough without them." There was a hint of bitterness in his statement.

"Are you challenging me?" There was a slamming sound, as if Reece had flattened his palms on his desk. "Because it fucking sounds like it. I'm alpha, I make the decisions. You don't like it, you can leave."

"I'm not challenging you." Ben's voice was more subdued now, but anger still laced his words. "And I trust you to make the right decisions. But it's not right that you have to mate her."

"Ben—"

"No! You should be with Sybil. She's strong, the kind of mate you deserve."

When Reece didn't immediately respond Alyssa felt the growing silence like a blow. She knew she wasn't the strongest wolf, not physically. But she'd thought there was something between her and Reece—and more than just physically. Weren't mates or intended mates supposed to defend each other? But maybe he really was just mating her out of a sense of duty. The thought of that made everything inside her go icy.

"Look, Ben, if things were different maybe I'd be with Sybil. But they're not. I'm mating with Alyssa to solidify the relationship between our packs. So you need to deal with it."

Alyssa swallowed back the sudden knot in her throat. His response hadn't been particularly horrible, but it still hurt. He'd said pretty much what their mating was originally supposed to be; a unification of the packs.

She'd been prepared to fight the mating until she'd met him. God, she felt so stupid and naïve, thinking they might have had something more together. Clearly the last three weeks they'd spent together had meant way more to her than him.

Which…wasn't his fault. If he didn't feel the same way about her she couldn't blame him. You couldn't help who you were attracted to. And sure, he was attracted to her, that much she could tell. But his words to Ben had been so cold and casual. Maybe all their conversations and time spent together had just been him putting in his duty, doing what his title of alpha commanded of him.

Reece saw her as a business decision. She didn't care if it was stupid, she wanted a mating based on more than that. More than pack responsibility. She wanted what her parents had had. Her mother had died giving birth to her, but her father had never gotten mated again because he'd loved her mother with everything in him and had never gotten over her death. And whenever he talked about her mom it was with love and adoration. Alyssa wasn't going to settle for less than that.

Feeling foolish and more than just a sting to her pride, she looked down at the ball cap in her hand, her fingers clenching around the soft material. She didn't care that it was pretty much a done deal as far as her father and Reece were concerned. She'd figure a way out of this mating no matter what.

Iciness invaded her veins as she realized the conversation between the two males had stopped. She wasn't going to wait around until either of them saw her. Moving swiftly she backtracked the way she'd come, leaving through the front door with a quietness she knew rivaled any wolf's stealth, even her father's. She'd learned young that if she wanted to get out from under the watchful eye of her packmates, she had to be sneaky about it.

Reece's pack lived in a quiet subdivision on the outskirts of a small but thriving South Carolina town. They owned all the houses in the neighborhood so there was no risk of any humans seeing big wolves running around. Not to mention the pack owned a hundred acres of forest that surrounded the neighborhood that they never planned to develop.

Right about now she wanted to strip and go running through the woods, but shook the instinct off. Her wolf just wanted to protect her, but she needed to figure out what she planned to do about Reece.

All she knew was, she wasn't staying here. Not after what she'd just heard.

She and her father were supposed to head back to their territory tomorrow so she'd just bide her time until then. Once they were home she'd tell him that the mating was off. He'd be angry, sure, but he'd get over it.

No way was she forcing Reece into a mating he didn't want. Wolves mated for life and it wouldn't be fair to either of them. And she wasn't ashamed to admit that she wanted love and a lasting partnership. She refused to settle for less.

CHAPTER ONE

Reece tried to reign in his temper as he strode up the front walk to Kayne Clare's house. He was in another alpha's territory. A much older alpha. And probably more powerful. It wasn't as if they'd ever come to blows, but with how Reece felt at the moment, that might happen today.

He slammed his knuckles against the front door, pounding on it harder than necessary. Unlike the more modern housing he and his pack lived in, Kayne's pack lived in a historic neighborhood in Oak Falls. It was only two towns over from Reece's.

The Clare pack owned land outside of Oak Falls where their pack ran when necessary. When they moved in a couple decades—as all shifters had to do in order to hide their slower aging from humans—he knew that Kayne would hold onto his land. It would be 'sold' to a holding company of sorts but would remain in Kayne's or the pack's possession. The male was smart, powerful and right now he was keeping Alyssa away from Reece.

Which meant things were about to get violent.

The door was wrenched open a few seconds later to reveal a pissed off-looking Kayne. Just as tall as Reece, the male had jet black hair he kept cropped close to his head. Wearing jeans, a T-shirt and no shoes, everything about him was tense. His dark eyes narrowed on Reece. "You have a death wish?"

Yeah, Reece definitely should have called the alpha first before entering his territory, but he wanted to see Alyssa and wasn't giving Kayne a chance to lie to him again. He was just lucky no one else in the Clare pack had seen him first. Well, maybe not lucky because if someone had challenged him, he had no problem taking out his aggression on someone right now. He ignored the question. "Where is she?"

Kayne's jaw tightened and for a long moment Reece thought he might actually attack. Then the other alpha surprised him and stepped back slightly. "We're not having this conversation out here."

Reece followed Kayne inside. The subtle sweet honeysuckle scent of Alyssa filled the house but he could tell she wasn't there. He knew she had her own place anyway, but he wasn't sure of her address. The disappointment that punched through him was stark and consuming. Nearly a week ago she'd called him and told him she didn't want to mate him and that was that. She'd been so formal about it and nothing he'd tried to say had been able to convince her to give them a chance. To be fair, she'd pretty much hung up on him after saying she was done with him.

Her words played in his mind, making his wolf edgy. *"Thank you for being gracious enough to host my father and me in your territory, but after meeting in person I've realized we won't suit each other. I'm sure this is a relief to you as well. I hope you find the right mate."* She'd said some other perfectly polite garbage in a neutral tone but he'd tuned it all out. After the words "we won't suit each other" had filtered through his brain he'd nearly lost it.

"Where. Is. She." He managed to get the words out through gritted teeth.

"I don't know." Kayne's entire body was stiff as he said the words.

"What?"

"I...don't know where she is. She left a week ago."

It took a long moment for Reece to digest what Kayne had said, to read the actual fear on the other alpha's face. As far as Reece knew, Kayne had always kept a close eye on his only daughter. She was basically considered a princess to the pack. Immediate worry for her sliced through him. His wolf clawed furiously, not liking this news one bit.

Before he could respond, Kayne jerked his chin to the left. "Come on, I need a drink."

A dozen questions were on the tip of his tongue, but he held himself in check. He'd get his answers. More than anything, he wanted to see Alyssa. The three weeks he'd spent with her had been the best of his life. She was like a ray of sunshine and he refused to live without her. Not when he knew that she wanted him too. Of that he had no doubt. Hell, he was the one who'd had to put the brakes on when they'd been kissing.

Because if he hadn't, he'd have taken and claimed her right on his living room floor. She deserved a longer courting than that. She deserved better than him, but he was too selfish to walk away from her. His wolf had decided that she was his before they'd ever spoken two words to each other, and once he'd met her, he agreed too. He had no clue what had gone wrong between them.

Her last night in his territory, she'd been withdrawn from him, but then she'd given him a gift. A vintage baseball hat for his favorite team. It had been so damn thoughtful, so like her. Something had been off with her though and he should have pushed to find out what it was. Feeling as if he was on autopilot, he followed Kayne into a huge kitchen bright from all the sunlight spilling into it.

"Sit," Kayne ordered.

Reece wanted to pace, but did as the other alpha said. He watched as the male pulled out an expensive bottle of single malt whisky from a cabinet. Kayne poured two glasses before joining Reece at the center island.

He slid it to Reece and to his surprise, he saw the slightest tremble in Kayne's hands. Shit. If Kayne was that worried, this was bad.

Ignoring the drink, he slid off the chair. Screw feigning civility. "Kayne—"

"She's okay. That much I know."

The words took away some of his fear, but not much. "How do you know?"

"She's texted me multiple times over the last week just to check in and assure me she's okay. But she disabled the locator on her phone so I can't even track her." The last part came out as a surly grumble.

"Alyssa wouldn't leave you like that." Reece had gotten to know her during their time together, so he knew without a doubt that she'd never hurt her father.

"She…" Kayne scrubbed a hand over his face. "We argued. Badly. She wanted out of the mating to you and I told her she was being immature, that this was the right thing. I've never seen her get so mad before. She shouted at me, something she's never done. I yelled back and fuck, I made her cry." He collapsed on one of the chairs. "She was gone the next morning."

"She was the one who wanted out of the mating?"

The alpha's mouth pulled into a thin line. "Yeah."

The knowledge was like a silver dagger to Reece's gut. He sat again and picked up the tumbler. He downed it in one swallow, savoring the burn of the liquid. "I didn't hurt her," he said, maybe more to convince himself than Kayne. He'd been so careful with her. Hell, they'd literally only kissed a few times. It had been intense and he'd wanted way more, but he'd never truly touched her. He hadn't trusted himself to stop and it had been clear she wouldn't have.

Kayne snorted. "I know that. It's the only reason you're alive. Something was wrong, she wouldn't tell me what. Just that she didn't want to mate."

Reece started to respond when he heard the sound of the front door opening. He scented a wolf, probably female, a few seconds before a tall, striking blonde strode into the kitchen.

She looked between the two of them, her eyes going cold as they landed on Reece. He'd never met her before so the coldness surprised him. Not that he cared about some random female.

"Is everything okay?" she asked Kayne, her expression softer as she looked at the alpha.

He nodded. "Yeah. Just worried about Alyssa."

"God, Kayne, she's fine. She just needed some space." The blonde shook her head, dismissing Kayne's words so quickly it was clear she knew where Alyssa was or at least had a good idea.

The other alpha picked up on that fact as soon as Reece did. Reece wanted to grill the female, but this wasn't his territory, and he wasn't sure of the relationship between Kayne and her.

Kayne's gaze narrowed, all worry from earlier gone, and pure alpha back in his gaze. "Where've you been the last week, Ember?"

The blonde shrugged and glanced at the whisky bottle with interest. "Busy. Have you forgotten your manners? Aren't you going to offer me a drink?"

"You don't drink whisky."

"I wouldn't say no to a twenty-year old single malt."

"Damn it, Ember!" He stood now, advanced on the female—who didn't back down an inch. "You know where she is?"

She crossed her arms over her chest, arched a defiant eyebrow. "Yes."

It was as if all the air was sucked out of the room with her response.

"And you didn't tell me?" Kayne's voice was low and deadly.

"You didn't ask. And I'm still not telling you."

Something electric sparked between the two of them. Even Reece could see it was sexual tension. He didn't give a shit what was going on though.

He forced himself to stay in his seat when all he wanted to do was get up and shake the female, to force an answer out of her. "Is she safe at least? Protected?"

Ember looked at him then, her eyes glinting with surprise. "You care?"

"Of course I care!" He'd gone too long without seeing her, without touching her or hearing her sweet laugh. And he'd thought she cared about him too.

"Hmm." She looked back at Kayne then. Even though she was tall, the alpha was taller so she had to look up. "On what planet did you think it would be a good idea to force a mating on your daughter?"

Kayne growled, but not at her bold question, it was more of a sound of frustration. "I wasn't trying to force her. I won't be around forever and I wanted her mated with someone strong, someone who would always take care of her. When Reece came to me about courting her—"

The blonde's head swiveled to Reece, then back to Kayne. "When did this happen?"

Reece wanted to know who the hell this female was that she was able to ask so many questions of the alpha without reprimand. But if it got him the answers he wanted, he'd tell her anything she wanted.

"About a month before Alyssa and Kayne came to my territory," he said before Kayne could respond.

Frowning, the female stepped back then moved around Kayne and grabbed the bottle. "Wait, there's no way you met her before then. She'd have told me."

Reece rubbed the back of his neck, suddenly uncomfortable. He'd seen Alyssa out shopping in a neighboring town before he knew who she was. His wolf had woken up and taken interest immediately. He'd been about to approach her until he spotted what looked like two bodyguards hovering nearby. After some research he'd discovered exactly who she was. So he'd approached Kayne about courting her.

Reece had never thought the older alpha would decree some sort of arranged mating. Not that he'd argued, because he'd wanted Alyssa with every fiber of his wolf.

"I didn't say we met. I just saw her."

"Then he came to me about courting her. I was the one who decided to implement the arranged mating." Kayne took the tumbler Ember had just poured and downed the contents.

"You're an idiot," she muttered, but with no heat as she turned to Reece. She looked at him hard, her gaze assessing. "Do you want Alyssa to strengthen your pack, or for her?"

"Her." God, he didn't give a shit about strengthening his pack. They already had a solid foothold in their territory and that wasn't changing. He'd told a few annoying packmates that was why he was mating with her, but soon everyone would see she was his.

If she'd just give him a chance.

"You actually sound like you're telling the truth. I need a few days to think about it before I tell you though."

His wolf instinct had him stepping forward before he'd realized he'd even moved.

Kayne moved lightning fast, yanking Ember behind him as she yelped in surprise. Kayne's wolf flared in his eyes and that was when Reece realized this was more than just sexual tension between him and the female. The alpha hadn't claimed her yet, otherwise Reece would have been able to scent him on her, but he definitely wanted to.

"She told you a few days," Kayne growled, the sound more animal than human.

"Fine. You know how to reach me," Reece said through gritted teeth. Not that he didn't already have two of his packmates trying to track her through other means. Sneaky? Yep. He'd hunt his little mate down any way he could. Then he'd convince her they were meant to be together.

Without another word he stalked from the kitchen and exited the house. As soon as he made it to his truck, he was calling his guys again, checking on their progress. He wasn't going to wait for one of Alyssa's packmates to tell him where she was.

* * *

"What was that?" Ember asked, her voice breathy and far too seductive for Kayne's sanity.

He took a deep breath, forced his wolf under control before he turned around to face her. It was becoming harder and harder to control his wolf around her. After his mate died almost three decades ago, he'd never thought he'd have the desire to mate again. And not to someone so young. She was thirty, but compared to his two hundred it felt wrong. At least that was what he'd been telling himself the last twelve months. The excuse was getting old though.

"You don't get to ask the questions," he murmured, finally turning to look at her. "You've been sitting on Alyssa's whereabouts for the past week, when you knew I was worried?"

She squirmed slightly and glanced away for a second. "It's not like I've seen you the past week, so how would I *know* you've been worried?"

"Don't be a smartass." He grabbed one of her hips in a purely dominating gesture, tugged her to him.

Her gaze flew to his, her eyes wide with surprise and... there was definite lust in the air. From both of them, not just her. He was exhausted trying to hide his reaction to her.

"Who've you been with the past week?" He could try to tell himself he had a right to know since he was her alpha, but it wasn't his business who Ember spent time with. She was a grown wolf and as far as he knew, she hadn't taken any lovers in the pack. For that he was grateful. Meant he wouldn't have to kill one of his packmates.

"None of your business." Her expression was more confused than defiant.

He sucked in a sharp breath, inhaling her sweetness. Leaning down, he ran his nose along the column of her neck.

She went completely still before her long, elegant fingers settled on his chest and he could feel her trembling. From lust or fear, he couldn't tell. Maybe a bit of both. Not that she could be afraid he'd ever hurt her. He'd rather cut off a limb. But he'd never touched her like this before. Even if he'd wanted to.

"Tell me," he murmured.

"No." She shoved at his chest. Hard. The action took him by surprise more than anything.

He didn't step back, but he lifted his head, looked down at her.

Her breathing was erratic. "I never thought you were cruel."

"Cruel?" He blinked in surprise, unable to stand the sudden tears shimmering in her gaze. God, he'd made two females he cared about cry in the last week. What the hell was wrong with him?

For the first time in years panic invaded his veins. Shifters in his pack didn't generally cry, they usually just took out their aggression or whatever by shifting and going for a run. Or fighting. He didn't know how to handle this.

"Using my attraction to you against me is unnecessary," she whispered as she wrapped her arms around herself. Clearly protecting herself from him. "I'll tell you where she is, I just… promised her I wouldn't. I don't want to lie."

That was when he realized Ember thought he'd been asking about Alyssa's whereabouts again.

A brief burst of shame filled him that he hadn't even been thinking about his daughter's location. Because the truth was, if she was in danger, Ember would have already told him. So he knew she was safe. All he'd been thinking about was who Ember had been spending time with. "I wasn't even thinking about her," he admitted, moving in on her, crowding her until he had her pinned against the center island.

Her tears dried as she stared at him with a hint of confusion and yeah, lust. "What?"

"I just wanted to know if there was some pup I should challenge." Even the thought of her with another male made him insane. She'd just returned to the pack a year ago and he'd been fighting his feelings and attraction the entire time. She was strong, smart and funny. He adored everything about her.

"Wait... *what*? Is this you being jealous?"

He watched her for a long, hard moment. The confusion rolling off her was real. For the last year she'd pushed his buttons and he'd let her. Hell, she was the only one in the pack he let get away with talking to him the way she did.

And others had certainly noticed. Probably why none of the males had made a move on her. He might not have actually claimed her, but in one sense he had. Now it was time to man up. "Yes."

When her eyes widened, he continued. "I want you, Ember. Have since you moved back. I won't settle for something casual so understand this, I'm possessive, stubborn, set in my ways, and have a lot of years on you. And I've got a lot of responsibility I deal with every day, something you know. You need to think about what you want, decide if a future with me is something you can handle because if we cross the line, it'll be for life." He wasn't admitting that he loved her just yet, because damn it, he couldn't say the words. He couldn't face her rejection.

Before she could respond, he spun on his heel and stalked from the room—and his house. He needed to shift and run. Because being around her and not claiming her was making his wolf go nuts.

CHAPTER TWO

Shelving the guilt that had been a constant companion the past week, Alyssa dropped her duffle bag next to her and knocked on her friend Charlie's front door.

Seconds later it flew open and she found herself pulled into a tight, welcoming hug. "I can't believe you're here!"

Alyssa laughed lightly, relief invading her veins in a slow, smooth crawl. After a week of traveling she was glad to be in Kincaid territory, a place she felt safe and welcome. Stepping back, she eyed her friend's long, dark hair. "You grew it out."

She fingered the strands, grinned. "Yeah, needed something different. Come on, let's get you inside." Charlie grabbed Alyssa's bag before she could stop her friend.

"I've got a suitcase in my car too." Not that she needed anything from it right now. After a day of driving she just wanted to kick her feet up and catch up with her old friend.

She snorted. "I figured you didn't pack this light. So, you want to tell me why you're here?"

"I just needed a break from my pack, that's all," Alyssa said, trailing after her down a hallway lined with beach-themed black and white prints and a few pictures of Charlie with her various packmates.

The hallway opened up into a huge open living room with floor-to-ceiling windows overlooking the Gulf Coast. Charlie was part of the Kincaid pack who lived in Orange Beach, Alabama. Alyssa knew the pack did well for themselves and owning beach front property was pricey anywhere. But the Kincaid pack owned the entire condominium she was now in.

The way the place was built each packmate had an ocean view. Unlike a lot of condos she'd been in, she noticed that when she'd headed up the stairs to Charlie's place all the hallways were glassed in instead of open. And they only had one main gated entrance with a high wall blocking the parking lot. The extra privacy made sense for a shifter pack.

"No way. You don't get off with that easy answer." Charlie dropped Alyssa's bag next to one of the microfiber couches and continued on to one of the sliding glass doors. The calming sound of ocean waves filled the room as she opened it.

When Alyssa stepped out onto the patio she saw that Charlie had a plate of cheese, crackers and stuffed mushrooms filled with some sort of cheesy mix that smelled delicious. And there was a bottle of wine. "I could kiss you right now."

"I've got vodka too, in case you needed it," Charlie said on a laugh.

Alyssa collapsed on one of the seats at the mosaic table. "I think wine's good." She'd been on the road for a week, stopping at various places and basically just enjoying the privacy away from her pack. She'd checked in with her dad via text and had been calling some of her packmates so they knew she was okay. She didn't want anyone to worry, but after the blowout with her father, she'd known space and time away were the only way she'd get past everything.

Charlie opened the wine bottle, poured them both glasses before sitting too. "Talk."

"My dad and I got in a pretty big argument." Even the thought of it made her throat tighten. She knew she was probably being a baby, but he'd never yelled at her before. Not once. And it had come as a shock. Her reaction annoyed her and she'd realized that if he was going to see her as an adult, she was going to have to make her own damn decisions. She never should have even entertained the idea of an arranged mating. She should have said no before they went to O'Shea territory. But she'd wanted to make her father happy.

She cleared her throat when Charlie didn't respond. "He wanted me to get mated to an alpha and I disagreed. Sort of. It's complicated. Anyway, when I told him I was backing out of the mating he wasn't happy."

Charlie's dark eyes widened. "Wait, your dad tried to force you to get mated?"

"Not exactly. He set up this arranged mating—"

"What!"

Ignoring her friend's cry of outrage, she snagged one of the stuffed mushrooms and popped it into her mouth. When she'd swallowed she looked at Charlie again, who was staring expectantly. "So he set up this arranged mating that I wasn't planning to go through with—until I met my intended mate." She felt so pathetic even admitting it out loud but if she couldn't be honest with her friends then she needed new ones. "I thought maybe we might have a chance at happiness."

Alyssa wasn't going to get into all the sweet things he'd done for her or the long conversations they'd had late into pretty much every evening for three weeks because it didn't matter. He felt differently about her. "But it turned out I was just a business deal to him. So I told my dad I didn't want to mate with him, we fought, and I left the next morning."

"First, I'm surprised your dad of all people would have pushed an arranged mating, given his relationship with your mom."

Alyssa nodded. She still couldn't wrap her mind around her dad's reaction. Lately he'd been edgy though, snapping at packmates. He was still fair, but his temper had seemed shorter the last few months. She wasn't sure what was going on with him. Well, she had an idea, but wasn't positive. "I know."

"Second, whoever this dickhead is who didn't want you for you—"

"He's not a dick."

Charlie snorted. "Anyone who thinks of you as a business deal, is a dick in my book. And I'm your friend so I get to be childish and mock him and his definitely small penis."

Alyssa snickered into her wine. She was pretty sure Reece wasn't small anywhere, but Charlie's words made her laugh. She'd met Charlie in college and given that they were both shifters, they'd bonded pretty quickly. Charlie was older and had taken

Alyssa under her wing more or less. She'd been a senior when Alyssa had been a freshman so they'd really only spent one year hanging out but she'd visited Charlie in Kincaid territory since graduating and vice versa. "Well, I wouldn't know about that."

"Good, at least you didn't sleep with him." She nodded once in approval. "Makes it a lot easier to get over a guy if you haven't sampled the goods."

At the faint sound of a knock, Alyssa glanced at the open sliding glass door. "Are you expecting someone?"

"Grant said he'd stop by."

"Oh, right." Charlie's alpha was giving her passage into his territory, no strings attached. She'd met him on more than one occasion when she'd visited Charlie and was thankful he was being so generous. Not that she expected less from the male.

Charlie popped up from her seat and disappeared inside with a supernatural quickness. Alyssa stood and smoothed her hands down her cashmere sweater and jeans. She felt a little grungy after the day of driving and wished she'd had time to freshen up. Especially since she figured she'd be getting to meet the alpha's new mate. Alyssa would be lying if she said she wasn't curious about the human female who'd made two-hundred year old Grant Kincaid fall hard.

Seconds later Grant and Alyssa strode onto the patio. Wearing jeans and a T-shirt didn't take away from the aura of authority that surrounded the dark-haired alpha. Just like Reece and her father, he seemed to carry an innate sense of power like a custom-made jacket. It wrapped around the male, letting any supernatural being know he wasn't a male to mess with. Well, unless you wanted your ass kicked.

Right now he was all smiles. "Hey, Alyssa. Glad to have you back in my territory." He gave her a quick hug and a kiss on the forehead.

Shifters were all about touch, but not all alphas were as friendly as Grant. Yeah, she'd definitely made the right decision coming here. She had down time to breathe without being hassled by her pack. "Thanks for having me. Listen, my dad doesn't know I'm here and—"

"He does now. Don't worry about it, he's glad you're here. Well, he's glad you're safe."

"You told him?"

"No. I got a call about ten minutes ago from him wanting to confirm you were here."

"Oh." She bit her bottom lip. "Did he sound mad?"

Grant snorted and shrugged. "He was a little surly but you're his kid. He's fine now that he knows where you are."

"I won't cause you any grief by being here?" That had been her main concern. If it would cause any strife between the two packs she would just leave.

"No. Just relax and enjoy yourself while you're here. I think... your father felt bad about something." There was a question in his gaze though he didn't outright ask.

No way was she delving into any of that. "Okay then." She *would* enjoy herself. "Thank you again for letting me stay. When do I get to meet your mate?"

His expression softened immediately. "She's working now but I know she's got a girls' night planned tomorrow if you—"

"We're in," Charlie interjected, slinging an arm around Alyssa's shoulders. "I'm showing my girl a good time while she's here."

Grant scrubbed a hand over his face. "Just keep her away from Sarah. I don't want you guys getting into trouble."

Charlie laughed and though Alyssa had no idea who Sarah was, she definitely wanted to meet her now. After Grant let himself out, Alyssa turned to her friend. "You still cut hair?"

"Every now and then," she said, picking up a slice of cheese and a cracker.

"I need a change."

Charlie's dark eyes gleamed. "I know just the cut for you, especially with your cheekbones."

"Good." It was beyond time for something new.

CHAPTER THREE

Two days later

As he parked at the newly renamed Kincaid Beach Resort, Reece knew he was basically risking death by entering another alpha's territory. It didn't matter that he was friendly with Grant Kincaid, he was still in the male's territory without permission. This could be seen as an act of aggression and disrespect. But the other alpha wasn't answering Reece's calls. Which wasn't like him, so it left Reece no choice.

He'd gotten word from Kayne that Alyssa was in Orange Beach and safe. While that had soothed some of the edges, he was still feeling unnaturally agitated. Now that he'd gotten a taste of the sweet female, he didn't want to let her go. If she truly didn't want to be with him after they talked, he'd walk away, but he'd sensed her hunger and need for him. Then it was like a switch had flipped between them.

The night of the Halloween festival he'd found her with some of his packmates at one of the local bars, but she hadn't been having a good time. She'd pasted on a big smile for everyone, but it hadn't reached her eyes. And that fake smile had remained in place for him.

Something his wolf hadn't liked. It was as if she'd put some sort of wall between them and he couldn't figure out why. Then she'd given him that gift and he'd thought maybe he'd been paranoid. But she hadn't been interested in spending any time with him that night. It had been subtle but she'd made an excuse about having to pack and get up early the next day. Looking back he realized he should have questioned her about what was going on. But they were still in that getting-to-know-you phase and he hadn't wanted to come off as, well, an alpha.

After finding parking, he headed through the front doors of the hotel. As he passed a young male wolf of about twenty—and received a snarl—he knew that Grant was likely already being contacted about Reece's presence.

Good.

He ignored the snarl and the fact that the male was following him, and headed right up to the front desk where a wolf in a dark suit and a female were talking.

The male turned before Reece had reached it, his green eyes sparking with not exactly anger, but annoyance. He murmured something to the woman then rounded the gleaming wood counter.

"Who the hell are you? And what are you doing in Kincaid territory?" the male murmured, low enough for only him to hear. There were only a few humans in the lobby but the male was clearly being civil for them.

"Reece O'Shea. I'm here to see Grant. I've tried calling him, but he's not answering. It's an emergency."

The male didn't say anything, just tapped his ear and that was when Reece saw the earpiece. Even with his supernatural hearing he could only hear a male murmuring. Maybe they had some kind of filtering system.

After a second, the man gave an affirmative grunt, then jerked his jaw toward a set of elevators across the shiny lobby. "This way."

Reece didn't even bother with small talk or to ask who the man was, even if he did look as if he could be Grant's brother. But he knew the alpha didn't have one so they must be cousins or some other distant relation.

The male swiped his keycard over a sensor before the elevator jerked to life. They got off on the twelfth floor with the male motioning for him to get off first. It went against all his nature to let some unknown wolf be at his back, but this wasn't his territory and he was in the wrong. He had to tread carefully and respect where he was. Reece had been taking a chance coming here and it seemed he'd been right to head to this hotel first instead of the pack's compound. Unless of course this guy was just bringing him up here to fight him instead of to see Grant.

The male fell in step with Reece as they headed down a hallway with open doors and a low level of chatter. Not a floor with bedrooms, but offices. They passed an office with a distinctive feminine scent coming from it. When he glanced inside he saw floor-to-ceiling gold curtains pulled back against a wall of windows, an expensive looking rug and an antique but delicate-looking desk.

The male made a growling sound at Reece so he glanced away from the room. They stopped at the next door, which was open. Grant was leaning against the front of his desk, arms crossed over his chest.

"Shut the door when you leave," he murmured to the other male.

The wolf paused, gave Reece a hard look before following orders.

"You wouldn't answer my calls," Reece said, jumping right into it.

Grant's wolf flashed in his eyes. "So you think showing up in my territory is the smartest course of action?"

"Not particularly." But to see Alyssa he'd do it.

"Then why are you here?" Grant's wolf was front and center in his gaze.

Yep, he'd definitely pissed the other wolf off. "My intended mate is here. I want to see her." And talk to her, hold her, find out what had happened between them.

Grant didn't move an inch or seem particularly surprised by Reece's statement. "I'm not keeping anyone captive in my territory."

Which meant Alyssa was here on her own. Something he already knew. He balled his hands into fists at his side, took a steadying breath before unclenching them. "I know. I want to see Alyssa."

"Why?"

"Why do I want to see her? Are you kidding me? Why are you being such a dick?" They'd interacted a few times over the last few years at various alpha meetings across the country and Grant had always been decent. Hell, more than decent. They'd shared beers together. The older generation wasn't always like that.

The male lifted one shoulder in a non-answer. "Why do you want to see her?"

"Because she's supposed to be my mate!" There was a gaping hole in his chest without her. The three weeks he'd spent with her had been the best of his life. She was like this bright, shining star that had been ripped away from him. He was territorial as fuck and he wasn't letting her go.

"Because she'll be a good way to solidify a relationship between you and her father?" Grant sounded disgusted by the idea of a business arrangement.

"No. I don't care about that. I just care about her."

Grant tilted his head slightly, his eyes narrowing as his wolf disappeared from his gaze. "You're not lying." He let his hands drop and motioned to the seat in front of the desk before he rounded it and sat in his own chair.

"Of course I'm not lying. Is she okay?" Because that was all that mattered right now.

"She's more than fine. She's with friends. If you just want her for her, then why did she overhear you telling one of your packmates that you were mating her to strengthen your two packs?"

"Wh...shit." Reece rubbed a hand over the back of his neck, tension settling in his shoulders.

"So it's true?"

"No, it's not true..." Hell, it had to have been that last night when he'd been arguing with Ben. "She must have overheard me say some bullshit to Ben. I don't know how she heard, but..." He hadn't meant it in the least. "Ben's a hothead, I just wanted to get him off my back and finish my paperwork so I could get to Alyssa."

Grant gave him an "are you kidding me" look. "When it comes to your mate or intended mate, you don't make excuses to *anyone*. Ever."

"You're right." Shame filled him at the older alpha's words. It wasn't right, but he'd just wanted to keep the peace with one of his oldest friends.

Grant lifted an eyebrow. "I expected you to defend yourself."

"I screwed up." And now he wondered if Alyssa would even talk to him. Grant was right, when it came to mates, things were black and white. You always had their back no matter what. It didn't matter if she wasn't officially his yet. He should have treated her like she was.

"You're young and it's a forgivable offense."

Under other circumstances he might have taken offense at the "young" comment, but Grant was over two hundred and right now he actually felt like a pup. A stupid pup who'd screwed up with a female he wanted more than his next breath. "You think she'll forgive me?"

Grant snorted. "No idea. I heard all this second hand from one of my packmates."

"Who?"

"Charlie."

"Who's that?"

Grant's lips quirked, annoying Reece. "Who Alyssa is staying with."

His wolf clawed at him, irrationally jealous. She was staying with some male? Using all his alpha strength, he pushed back his wolf as best he could. His claws actually pricked his fingers but there was no one to fight except himself.

When he spoke he knew his wolf was in his eyes but there was no helping that. "Will you ask Alyssa to meet with me?" Despite his need to demand to see her, he had to do things right and apologize. Barging into where she was staying wasn't the best idea.

"I'll do one better. She's at the Crescent Moon Bar with Charlie and some others right now. I'm giving you safe passage in my territory as long as Alyssa doesn't ask me to kick you out and as long as you act... as civil as a male fighting his mating instinct can act. Don't hurt any males in my pack. If they challenge you, fine. You may fight back but not to the death. Keep it civil."

"You'll tell your pack I'm in town?"

He nodded. "I'll spread the word quickly. Max is at Crescent Moon now and I'm sure he'd be happy to see you anyway. Head over there, see your woman and apologize."

Something told him a simple apology wouldn't be enough, but he nodded. "Thank you."

"I know what it's like to screw up with my own female."

It was hard to imagine the older wolf doing that, but he just nodded and stood. As he made his way to the door, Grant stopped him.

"Charlie's a female. In case you were wondering." That was definite laughter in the male's voice now.

Reece didn't even care. The news that Alyssa was staying with a female and not a male was a balm to all the edginess that had invaded his veins. It was time to find his mate.

The drive to the bar took all of five minutes. By the time he got there energy and hunger hummed through him in an out of control rhythm.

Laughter and music drifted out from the open front door as he walked across the graveled parking lot. The neon sign above the beach bar was bright and welcoming. He scented shifters and humans as he grabbed the big brass handle of the heavy wooden door before it could close again.

The music seemed to crank up a hundred decibels when he stepped inside. The place was packed, three deep at both bars. The high-top tables were all full, someone was singing on a small stage in what was apparently karaoke night and—there, at the pool tables.

He moved farther inside but stuck to the shadows of a vintage pinball machine, using it to cover him as he drank in the sight of Alyssa.

She was in profile to him, her previously long inky black hair now a short bob around her face. His cock hardened at the sight of her. Her cheekbones seemed even sharper now and even though he couldn't see them, he could just imagine her bright blue eyes filled with laughter. She wore her emotions right out in the open. When her head fell back in laughter at something a petite blonde female said, the sound of it slid through him like warm honey.

Over all the other sounds he could pick out her voice, her laughter, anywhere.

He immediately spotted Max with a woman who looked similar to the first blonde. There were a handful of other wolves at a nearby table, some playing pool, others just talking.

When a dark-haired male sidled up to Alyssa, a hopeful smile on his face, Reece's claws automatically extended.

Inwardly cursing, he glanced around but no one was paying attention to him. He took a deep breath and got himself under control. When he looked over again he saw the male was leading Alyssa to a dance floor.

His first instinct was to go over there and pummel the shit out of the guy but he had no right. She looked like she was having fun too. That was the only thing that made him take a step back and leave. It cut deep that she was out having fun with another male when she wouldn't even talk to him. But he'd brought it on himself.

He wasn't going to ruin her night. Because right now wasn't about him. It was about her.

Once outside he called Grant. Tomorrow he'd start the official process of courting Alyssa again. He just had to make sure she'd answer the door when he stopped by.

CHAPTER FOUR

Reece waited until he saw Charlie leave the condo Alyssa was at. Thankfully Grant had come through and gotten his pack member out so Reece could talk to Alyssa in private. All he wanted was a few minutes alone with her. Okay, he wanted a lot more than that, but he'd settle for talking.

Instead of using the elevator, he hurried up the stairs and pressed the doorbell. Alyssa was a morning person so he had no doubt she'd be awake.

Seconds later the door opened and her bright blue eyes widened in pure shock. There were enough varying scents on this floor that she might not have caught his scent outside. Her newly shortened hair was tousled, making her look like he imagined she would after a night of hot sex.

He pushed the distracting thought aside. "Hey, Alyssa." He handed her the drink he'd bought on the way here.

Blinking once, she took it as if she was on autopilot.

He wasn't ashamed to admit that he was going to use her shock to his advantage. Stepping closer, he moved so that he was in the doorway with her—and she couldn't slam the door in his face. "I'd like to talk to you."

She shook her head once, as if coming back to herself. "What are you doing here?"

"I missed you." A simple truth.

Alyssa inhaled slightly, disbelief and confusion warring in her beautiful eyes. Probably because she scented he was being honest. Her own scent put off a mix of emotions he couldn't wade through. "You can't just barge into this territory—"

"I've already talked to Grant. He knows I'm here with you. It's why he called Charlie away. So we could talk." Reece left out the part about Grant kicking him out of the territory if Alyssa wanted him gone. No need to give her ammunition.

"Oh." She ran a hand through her hair, agitation clear in her expression, but then she sighed. "Fine. Close the door behind you. We'll talk on the patio." She turned from him, the soft sway of her ass mesmerizing for a long moment.

Following after her was definitely not a hardship, even if she was clearly angry at him. Once outside with her, he set the small brown paper bag on the table as she sat on one of the chairs.

Her body language was closed off, all her muscles pulled tight as she crossed her arms over her chest.

"I brought you cranberry muffins," he said, motioning to the bag. "And yours is a cappuccino, not regular coffee."

"You remembered." For a moment her expression softened, but just as quickly a neutral mask was back in place. It was so unlike the woman he'd gotten to know those three weeks. The woman who'd told him that he needed to smile more.

"I owe you an apology. I know you overheard my conversation with Ben and I never should have said what I did."

She lifted her shoulders, the action jerky. "You can't help how you feel. It's not like we made any promises to each other."

That wasn't exactly true, but he didn't point out that he'd made some dirty promises to her. He'd loved getting her to blush and when he'd discovered telling her what he wanted to do to her did just that, he'd been explicit. Even if he hadn't gotten to follow through yet. "I care for you, Alyssa. What I said to Ben was a lie. I wanted to get him off my back but that's no excuse." The male had been driving him nuts for weeks since Alyssa had arrived in their territory and Reece had been at his breaking point. Ben was a good packmate but sometimes he was like a pup. "I don't give a shit about aligning our packs. I just care about you and I'm sorry I didn't show that the way I should have."

"I appreciate the apology." She glanced away from him, the soft breeze ruffling her hair. God, he wanted to run his hands through it, to cup the back of her head as he claimed her mouth. "But I don't want to mate you. Not now and not in the future. Mates are supposed to have each other's backs. Always."

It was the same thing Grant had said to him last night. It was one of those black and white things in the shifter world. "I know, and I'm sorry. I'm asking for another chance. Let me make it up to you. Please."

She looked at him now, wariness in her gaze. He was struck by how vulnerable she appeared. Before Alyssa he'd always been with tougher, more experienced females. She was softer and sweeter than anyone he'd known. He hated that he'd put that look in her eyes. "No."

The sense of finality in the one word slammed into him. She didn't give him an excuse or reason—not that it wasn't obvious—just a no. Well, he wasn't giving up. He'd committed a cardinal sin as far as shifters were concerned by not defending his would-be mate but that didn't mean he was walking away.

Especially not when he saw her gaze dip to his lips for the briefest moment. Hunger flared bright in her eyes before she glanced away, refusing to look at him.

As an alpha, he knew when to retreat and regroup so he stood and nudged the bag closer to her side of the table. "They're probably still warm."

He'd be back tomorrow morning and every morning after until he convinced her to go for a run with him, or out to breakfast. Whatever. Something to just spend time with her. Today wasn't that day though. He could see it in the firm set of her jaw. It was hard to leave, but it was his only option without risking alienating her further.

"Thanks for the coffee and muffins," she murmured, clearly not going to walk him out.

Not that he blamed her. At the sliding glass door, he paused. "You were wrong before. I did make a couple promises to you that I intend to keep."

When her brow furrowed, he resisted the urge to cover the distance between them and smooth out the frown lines.

"I promised to make you come all over my tongue and fingers and to give you so much pleasure you'll crave me when I'm not with you."

"Reece," she gasped out, nearly knocking her drink over. Her tone was a mix of shock and a little arousal. The first real show of emotion since he'd arrived. Her cheeks flushed and that was definitely desire that sparked in her bright gaze.

The sight made him instantly hard, but he didn't say anything, just left through the open door. He hoped that gave her something to think about. God knew he'd certainly be thinking about it.

* * *

"Thanks," Alyssa said as Charlie slid her a bottle of water across the high-top table. She was already edgy enough, especially since Reece had walked into the bar twenty minutes ago. She didn't need any alcohol to rattle her brain. And with her shifter metabolism it would take a lot to get her even buzzed right now.

"You're still thinking about him," Charlie said with a grin, her voice low enough that no one else would be able to hear them. Not above the chatter of voices and music pumping through the speakers in the martini bar. Red and purple-hued overhead lights illuminated their table and the whole bar area they were in, giving everything a soft glow.

"So?" No need to deny it. Not when all she'd been able to think about today was Reece O'Shea, sexy alpha with a dirty mouth and sculpted body. Well, what she'd seen of it, but it was clear the male was built. Most shifter males were.

Charlie lifted a shoulder. "Hey, I'm impressed with the guy."

"You said he was a dick."

"He was a dick, but he also stormed into another alpha's territory to see you. You said yourself he wasn't lying about what you'd overheard. The fact that he was willing to face Grant's wrath just to see you is impressive."

"Yeah, maybe." Alphas could sometimes cover their scents depending on how powerful they were so it wasn't out of the realm of possibility that he'd lied and just covered his scent. But deep down she believed Reece. Which just confused her more. She'd never expected him to come after her and now that he was here, she felt all sorts of mixed up. She'd put him into this box in her mind, convinced herself he was one thing. Now... ugh, maybe she did need a drink.

"No maybe about it. Grant said Reece wasn't lying and he'd be able to tell."

"Oh, are we talking about your alpha?" A woman named Lauren asked as she slid onto one of the empty barstools, a new martini in hand. Petite with honey brown hair and big brown eyes, the jaguar shifter had mated Max McCray, the Kincaid pack's second-in-command a little over a year ago.

Alyssa had met Lauren and her cousin Ella for the first time last night and they were both incredibly sweet. "He's not *my* alpha."

"Oh, he's most definitely yours," Charlie said. "He's been watching you for the last twenty minutes as if he could do very, very wicked things to you."

Charlie and Lauren dissolved into giggles and Alyssa wondered just how much they'd had to drink. They'd all arrived at the Sunset Martini Bar a couple hours ago and while she'd been drinking mostly water in between dancing, the other two had been working on vodka martinis. With the exception of last night, it had been over a year since she'd been able to go out and enjoy herself like this. At home she worked a lot and while she loved her job she'd always found it hard to cut loose.

That had a lot to do with being the alpha's daughter. Everyone was always worried about keeping an eye on her, as if she was completely helpless. Or needed to be protected. She ran all the finances for the pack and did most of the scheduling for, well, everything pack related. She was basically an accountant/shifter party planner for the Clare pack. Right now she liked being basically anonymous.

Tingles traced up her spine, and even before she turned around she knew Reece was moving her way. That shouldn't excite her so much, but after his visit this morning he was all she'd been able to think about. Obsess about. Her nipples beaded tightly against her bra as his earthy, masculine scent grew stronger, invading all her senses.

Damn that male.

She turned to see where he was right as his heavy hand landed on her shoulder. When their gazes clashed she felt the heat of his dark stare all the way to her toes.

"Dance with me?" he asked quietly.

Before she could even formulate a response, her traitorous body was already moving into action, sliding off the stool and taking the hand he offered. Yeah, she wanted to press up against him, to feel his big arms wrap around her and hold her close. She was vaguely aware of her surroundings, the plush chairs set up in intimate groupings for people to talk and relax, another set of high-top tables before they reached a small but packed dance floor.

A smooth Latin jazz beat started as Reece pulled her into his arms. One hand slid to the small of her back as one grasped her hip. Not tight, but with enough pressure that she felt the possessiveness of his hold.

Swaying to the music, she linked her fingers behind his neck. It was a good thing she hadn't been drinking because looking into his mesmerizing gaze, she felt lightheaded as it was.

"You look beautiful," he murmured, his gaze never leaving hers.

She was pretty much powerless to look away. Not that she wanted to. Being in his arms had a rightness to it, as much as it annoyed her. "Thanks. You look pretty good yourself."

In dark jeans and a soft, dark gray sweater, he looked delicious. Of course he looked delicious no matter what. His lips quirked up slightly. "Thanks. I've been thinking about you all day."

She blinked at the admission, unsure how to respond.

Those wicked lips curved up again. "You want to know what I've been thinking about?"

"No." *Yes.* She cleared her throat, desperately needing to change the subject. "How's your pack doing without you?"

"They're fine. What about yours? I know they depend on you for a lot."

The fact that he knew that meant a lot. "I brought my laptop with me." She'd gotten a lot of emails—some under the guise of random questions even though she knew they'd been checking in on her for her father, but most of the stuff she did was easy enough to do online.

"Will you go running with me tonight?"

"Ah, no." Because she didn't trust herself to get naked with the male. Weak? Yep. And she had no problem admitting it. Plus she was a little nervous. The whole nude thing wasn't a big deal to the majority of shifters and for the most part, not to her either. But she'd never slept with a male before so getting naked with a male she wanted to have sex with was a lot different than just getting naked with packmates before a run. And going running with a shifter not part of her pack implied a certain amount of trust. You were at your most vulnerable during the change from human to wolf. They weren't there in the trust department yet. Maybe they'd never be.

He'd totally changed everything by showing up here. Knowing that he'd been lying to Ben soothed her hurt feelings but still, he was an alpha. She needed a male to be proud of her, to want to tell everyone that yeah, this is *my* female. Not just make an excuse for why he was mating her.

And that was the crux of it. His confession had pissed her wolf off way more than her human side. Wolves were very primal and he'd offended her, simple as that. She figured she'd be able to get past it, but not tonight.

A hint of frustration edged into his expression, highlighting the hard planes of his face. "You want to."

She wanted to trace her fingers over those lips. It was the only soft part about him. Finding her voice, she nodded. "I do."

"So why not come with me?" His voice dropped an octave and was it just her imagination, or did he put extra emphasis on the word *come?*

She couldn't very well say, *"Because if I see you naked I'll reveal myself to be weak, weak, weak—and jump your bones."* So she did the mature thing and shrugged.

His grip on her tightened and he pulled her closer so that her breasts pressed completely against him. She was wearing a sweater dress and high-heel boots. The boots gave her a few extra inches so she fit against him perfectly. She'd had way too many fantasies about what it would feel like to be pressed against him, skin to skin. The last time they'd kissed had been in his living room and she'd been ready to find out then.

Until he'd pulled back. She'd straddled him, had been grinding against him and he'd put the brakes on. The most insecure part of her wondered why but she'd been too afraid to ask. She'd worried she wouldn't like the answer. "So how long are you here?"

"As long as it takes to convince you to come back with me."

Shock rippled through her. "You can't…"

"I can't what?"

"Nothing." She glanced away from him.

"I don't like the scent of other males on you," he murmured, drawing her attention back to him.

She was surprised when his wolf flickered in his gaze for just a moment. That loss of control wasn't like him, at least not the male she'd gotten to know. "I haven't been with any other males—not that it's your business."

Was that relief in his expression? "You danced with some tonight." Not a question or an accusation. But he sounded agitated and his wolf showed again.

"So?"

"So, I don't like it."

She noticed he wasn't telling her not to dance with anyone else, just making a statement. The truth was, she wouldn't like the scent of another female on him either. Even the thought of it had her wolf clawing, ready to break free. Sometimes her animal side made her crazy. "I won't dance with anyone else tonight." The words were out of her mouth before she could analyze them or even think about stopping herself.

His eyebrows raised then something that looked a lot like triumph flickered in his dark eyes before it disappeared. As the song started to end, he cupped the side of her face with his big hand, his palm rough and callused. "You sure you don't want to run with me tonight?"

"I'm sure." *Liar, liar*, her inner voice shouted. She needed more time to think and when she was around him that seemed a difficult feat.

He didn't respond, just pulled her tighter to him in a completely dominant, possessive move as a new song started to play. She'd planned to make her way back to her friends after their dance but it seemed he wasn't content to let her go. Which was fine with her. She didn't want to let go of him either.

CHAPTER FIVE

Four days later

Alyssa's heart rate kicked up at the sound of a knock on the front door. It was Reece, no doubt. He'd been meeting her every morning and bringing her a cappuccino and breakfast the past few days like clockwork. He kept asking her to go for a run with him and she'd kept turning him down.

Her wolf, and okay her human side, wanted him to work for it a little. Work for her. Because there was no denying she wanted him. She wasn't certain she wanted to be an alpha's mate, but she wasn't going to ignore the attraction between them. She'd forgiven him for what he'd said but there was still a lot to consider if she started a relationship with him.

When she opened the door, sure enough Reece stood there with two to-go cups and a brown bag of blueberry muffins, if she scented right. She couldn't have stopped the smile that spread across her face if she'd wanted to. Seeing him in the morning was the right way to start any day. It touched her that he was trying to make amends without being pushy. Instead he was courting her, the way shifters tended to do when they wanted to mate.

"Morning," he murmured. His gaze dipped to her mouth, hunger flaring bright, as he handed her a cup.

"Morning yourself," she said, taking the bag from him. She set it on the entryway table before stepping out into the hallway with him. She pulled the door shut behind her. Charlie was still sleeping, and anyway and Alyssa wanted some alone time with him. "Feel like taking a walk on the beach?"

His gaze went molten hot as he nodded. The walk down to the beach was quiet, not too many people out this time of morning. Not with the chilly breeze coming up off the water. It didn't bother her though, not with her shifter blood. The weather was a lot different than where they lived too, so she was wearing a light sweater and jeans. She left her shoes by the end of the wooden walkway and dug her feet into the sand as they made their way down to the shoreline.

"If you want to shift, Grant said this stretch of beach is private," Reece said before taking a sip of his coffee.

"I'd rather just talk." She was to the point where her wolf trusted him enough to shift and be vulnerable, but she'd gone running with Charlie last night and was feeling pretty settled. Probably had something to do with being in Reece's presence because her shifter side had definitely forgiven him by now. She had too, but it was one thing to let go and another to truly trust that he'd support her no matter what. That was something she'd only know when and if he showed her.

"Good." He clasped her hand and linked his fingers through hers.

The sweet action took her off guard, but she liked it. "Can I ask you something personal?" It wasn't her business but it was something she needed to know.

"Yes."

She kept her gaze ahead, focused on the stretch of white sand and washed up seashells. "I don't have a lot of experience with pack life other than my own and…" This was a little awkward. Now that she'd started she wondered if she should even ask. "My father has never slept with any of the females in our pack. I assume he, well, finds… companionship elsewhere, but he doesn't sleep around." She knew it was partially because he'd been so broken when her mother died, but also because it could lead to a power imbalance.

"You didn't actually ask a question but I think I know what you're asking. Since I became alpha, I haven't slept with any females in my pack for probably the same reason as your father. There would be too much inter-pack fighting or a pack member could feel as if they had to sleep with me because of my position."

She was silent, digesting his words. It was something she wanted to know because if he had slept around and they mated, she would want to know who in the pack might have a grudge against her.

"I did sleep with some females in the pack before I became alpha," he continued. "But those have moved onto other packs since I took over."

She shouldn't feel relief at that, but experienced it all the same. "Was it hard taking over?" She'd only ever known her father as an alpha so wasn't sure what it would be like during a transition. And Reece was young for an alpha. Not that his age mattered. Power pulsed around him as if it were a tangible thing.

He paused and she liked that he took his time answering. "It was exhausting in the beginning. For about the first two months I was challenged almost every other day for authority. At first I simply dominated the other males in fights but didn't make my wins overkill. After two months..." He shrugged, trailing off.

He didn't need to finish though. She understood completely. He got tired of the challenges so he wiped the floor with those who continued to push him. Shifters, especially males, seemed to only respect physical strength. It was something that annoyed her about her species, but it was just the way things were.

"When I went to see your father I met a female named Ember," he continued. "Who is she to...you?"

Alyssa snorted. Ember had it bad for Alyssa's dad, but both of them were too cowardly to do anything about it. "She's one of my dearest friends but I think you really wanted to ask who she is to my father. If he can ever get his head out of his butt, he'll mate Ember."

Reece laughed, the rumbling sound soothing to every bit of her.

"I love your laugh," she said.

She felt him look at her, but she didn't meet his gaze, just kept their steady pace along the sand. Grant was right, this stretch was incredibly private and quiet. Seagulls and the crash of waves were the only sounds.

"I saw you, you know. Before I asked you and your father to my territory."

Now she glanced over at him. "You did?"

His dark eyes met hers. "I saw you shopping over in Waterstone. You had a couple bodyguards with you."

She hadn't seen him because Reece was the type of man she'd remember—the type any woman would remember. She wondered why he hadn't said anything before. "Oh… Did you know who I was then?"

He gave a small shake of his head. "No, but I wanted to know you. I would have talked to you too, but the males with you kept you pretty close. So I might have done a little research on you."

She raised her eyebrows.

To her surprise, his cheeks flushed. "I snapped a photo of you and had one of my guys see what he could find. And… I might have followed you and your guards to Clare territory. When I realized what territory you were going into it wasn't hard to find out who you were after that."

"So you pretty much stalked me?" Her mouth curved up as warmth invaded her. Maybe she should be freaked out but she wasn't.

He lifted a shoulder, completely unapologetic. "I wanted to talk to you. Full disclosure, I approached your father once I knew who you were. I asked him to visit my territory and to bring you. I made my intentions clear from the start. He came up with the arranged mating thing." His lips twisted in annoyance. "But I didn't stop him because the thought of waking up to you every day..." When he trailed off she realized he was nervous.

The thought of big, bad alpha Reece actually unsure of himself seemed wrong somehow. He might have screwed up before, but he'd been nothing but real with her since arriving in Orange Beach.

When he started to glance away, she stopped in her tracks and grabbed his shirt, tugging him down to her.

That was all it took. He slanted his mouth over hers, taking and claiming her lips with a fervent urgency. One hand slid around her waist, pulling her close and the other cupped the back of her head in a hard, dominating grip.

Reece was consumed with the need to claim Alyssa even if it was way too soon, at least for her. He knew what he wanted, what his wolf wanted, and he wasn't going to question the pull he felt for her.

But she'd been softening toward him the last four days. This morning when she'd given him that blinding smile he swore his heart had skipped a beat. Everything about this female called to him so that when he was with her all he could think was; *mine*.

She *was* his.

Right now he wanted to make good on one of those promises he'd made her. Using his shifter senses, he knew they were completely alone on the beach.

When she slid her fingers up his chest and clutched onto his shoulders, a growl tore from his throat. He loved the feel of her touching him, loved the taste of her. Now he wanted to taste more of her.

He clutched her ass, smiled against her mouth at her little yelp when he hoisted her up. She wrapped her legs around him without pause. He could feel her heart rate kick up as she held onto him.

Breathing hard, she pulled back to look at him. Her jet black hair was tousled around her face, her blue eyes bright. "What are you doing?"

"Do you trust me?"

"Yes." Her answer was instant, her voice breathless.

He glanced up and down the beach, saw no one. He'd have scented someone anyway, but the visual confirmed they were alone. Holding her tightly, he hurried up the sloping sand, using his supernatural speed to cover the distance quickly.

As he reached the top of a dune, he saw that it dipped down into another miniature valley. Oh yeah, the foliage and dunes created more than enough shelter. Before he'd taken a step down the dune, Alyssa nipped at his jaw, her teeth scraping against him before she followed it up with a string of kisses.

His erection pressed against his jeans, but he focused on Alyssa and her hot mouth as she continued a teasing trail down his neck. He wanted to feel her coming against his mouth and fingers.

"Alyssa," he murmured, collapsing against the sand with her on top of him.

She straddled him, scraping her teeth against his neck again. He rolled his hips once, then grabbed hers and flipped their bodies. It was impossible to give up control.

Eyes wide, she looked up at him as he settled on top of her. Her wolf flickered in her bright eyes for a moment and her pulse point was going wild.

"I want to see you," he murmured, inhaling deeply. The scent of her desire was intoxicating. No wonder mated males went all primal and possessive over their females. He never wanted her to have this reaction for anyone else. Only him.

She nodded, her breathing erratic.

He slid his hands to her waist and pushed up the hem of her sweater. The material was soft and light, but nothing was as smooth as her skin. Before he'd pushed it up higher than her stomach, she grasped the hem and tugged it off her.

There was a hungry gleam in her gaze, even if he could sense her nervousness. Not that she had anything to be nervous about.

The lacy purple bra she wore didn't hide much of anything. Reaching behind her, he unclasped it and when her hands went to cover herself, he grasped her wrists, held them still.

"Don't hide from me." Not ever. This female brought out every possessive and protective instinct he had.

Swallowing hard, she nodded. It made him wonder how much experience she had or if maybe it was because they were semi-exposed outside. But shifters usually didn't care about that. Hell, maybe it was just because it was him. "You want to stop, we stop. Okay?"

"Okay."

Knowing that she trusted him in this soothed all his ragged edges. Most of them. He was still keyed up, ready to bring her to a toe-numbing climax. He finished pulling her bra free and his cock kicked against his pants again as her breasts were completely revealed. Full, a little more than a handful, and tipped with light brown nipples, she was utter perfection.

Reece told himself to slow down, but he couldn't help himself. His head dipped and he sucked one hard bud into his mouth.

"Reece!" She arched into him, her fingers sliding in his hair as he stroked his tongue over her tight nipple.

She started grinding against him as he kissed and teased her. God, she was so reactive and they'd barely gotten started. When her hands moved from his shoulders down to his chest, he pulled back.

He could feel the intent in her movements. Right now he couldn't afford for her to touch his cock. Not if he wanted to be able to think. And he refused to take her for the first time in the sand at the beach. He wanted to bring her pleasure, but actually sinking inside her, feeling her tight body... no, that was something for when they were alone. Because he wanted to savor her for hours.

"This is just about you right now," he murmured, dropping a kiss to her lips. He gently tugged on the bottom one as her fingers dug into his chest muscles. When they finally made it to a bedroom, or a better flat surface than this, and he had all the time in the world, he was going to give her as much foreplay as she could stand. Because just her touching him now was making him crazy and he still had all his clothes on.

She made a protesting sound when he drew away, but when he nipped at her jaw, she settled down. As her body fully relaxed, he slid a palm down her flat stomach, unfastened the button of her jeans.

She practically melted under him, tightening her hold as he slid a hand down the front of her panties. More than anything he wanted to strip her bare but if she was completely naked in front of him, he wasn't sure how his wolf would react. He was barely hanging on as it was.

Make her come, bring her pleasure, he ordered himself. This was all about Alyssa.

"Reece," she gasped out when he rubbed his middle finger over her clit. Even without delving any farther between her folds, he felt her slickness.

It was all for him. That knowledge pierced through him. Her fingers dug into his shoulders, her claws flicking out just the slightest bit. He scented his own blood as she broke skin.

He welcomed the spark of pain, loved that he was pushing her to the edge so fast. "I want to feel you come," he murmured, kissing along the smooth column of her neck. He increased his stroking against her swollen clit, rubbing her in a steady rhythm.

With each caress, the more out of control her movements became. When he raked his canines against her pulse point, she took him by surprise. Crying out his name, she jerked against his hand before he'd even penetrated her.

"Reece," she moaned his name like a prayer as her orgasm rocked through her.

He kept teasing her until she made a mild protesting sound and released his shoulders. Withdrawing his hand, he licked the finger he'd been stroking her with.

Her cheeks went crimson as she watched him. Another blast of her lust rolled over him as he looked at her. In that moment he realized he'd never felt more content. His dick ached and he wanted inside her like he wanted his next breath, but he simply liked being with her.

Her lips were slightly swollen and her blue eyes were bright with satisfaction. He'd done that, put that look on her face. She almost looked as if she were coming out of a daze.

Unable to keep his mouth off her, he skated his lips over hers. "Thank you."

Laughing lightly, she said, "I think I should be saying that to you."

"I'm just glad you trusted me enough for this." Getting intimate in public wasn't for everyone, and even though this wasn't technically public, it was close enough.

Her cheeks flushed a darker shade of pink than they already were. "I hope we're not done?" The hopeful note in her voice was almost enough to make him shed his control and take her right here. It was clear she wanted to and he definitely did, but... he wanted more for her their first time.

"Have dinner with me tonight," he said instead.

Disappointment played over her features but she nodded and picked up her bra from the sand. "Why don't you want to…" She trailed off, looking away from him as she hooked her bra and grabbed her sweater.

"I smell a couple shifters nearby." They were far enough away that he wasn't worried about them seeing Alyssa, but close enough he scented them. He wouldn't risk being vulnerable like that in another wolf's territory. Because if he was vulnerable then it meant he'd be less equipped to protect Alyssa.

"Really?"

"Yeah," he murmured, pushing up on the dune so he could get a better view of who might be nearby. It was just as well because he was close to losing control. Taking a steadying breath, he forced his claws to retract.

"Okay but I'm going to return that favor later." She said the words in a rush.

When he looked back at her, she gave him a shy, almost unsure smile. Not for the first time he wondered how much experience she had. Not wanting her to ever question herself where he was concerned, he grinned. "Later we're both going to be naked and I'm going to hear you cry out my name when I'm inside you." Soon he hoped she'd be more open to mating him for good. It was clear she'd forgiven him and trusted him. He wanted to show her that he was playing for keeps. There wasn't anyone else he wanted but her.

She sucked in a sharp breath, but when she nodded and gave him the most wicked smile, he lost his own breath.

CHAPTER SIX

"Remember that thing you told me I'd love for a male to do to me?" Alyssa asked Ember by way of greeting when her friend answered her call.

"Yes! Tell me you finally let a guy go down on you!"

She laughed, unable to stop herself. "Well, it hasn't happened *yet,* but it's going to." Probably tonight. Earlier today when Reece had stroked her to orgasm, she'd wondered what it would feel like to have his mouth there as well. Ember had promised her that she'd love it but Alyssa had always wondered how she'd get over feeling self-conscious. Now she knew because she wanted Reece's hands and mouth all over her. She trusted him completely with her body.

"Don't tease me," Ember muttered. "I want to know when it *actually* happens."

"That's because you're a pervert. And it's why I love you."

"So... I'm assuming you're referring to *your* alpha? Did you guys make up?"

Alyssa wasn't going to deny that he was "her" alpha anymore because she'd started to think of Reece that way as well. "Yes, not that we were ever actually arguing." Not technically.

"And? Have you guys moved past kissing?"

"Yes."

"Are you going to make me beg for details?"

"Hmm," Alyssa murmured, looking at herself in the bedroom mirror. Reece would be picking her up in the next ten minutes and she still wasn't decided on what she was going to wear. She'd never cared about this stuff before. "No, but no details just yet." She and Ember had been friends growing up, then Ember moved away for school and then she'd traveled for years for her job after she graduated. Only in the past year had they become close again. While she shared everything with the other woman, Alyssa wanted to keep what had happened between her and Reece private. At least the actual details.

"Is he being good to you?"

"Yes."

"Okay, that's all that matters. He was pretty torn up looking for you. Barged right into our territory like he had a death wish."

"I heard you still wouldn't tell him where I was."

Ember laughed. "Yeah well, that's what friends are for. When are you coming home? Everyone misses you."

"I'm not sure yet." She missed her pack but she was still unsure about where things stood between her and Reece. Not that she was unsure of her feelings, but she wanted to take things slow. She had a feeling he wouldn't mind if she moved into his place when they returned to South Carolina, but she didn't know if that was too soon. She also wasn't sure if she wanted to move back to Oak Falls. Having freedom here in Orange Beach was refreshing, as if she could breathe freely for the first time in years. If she moved to Reece's territory she was afraid she'd lose that sense of freedom.

"It's nice not being smothered, huh?"

"I swear you're a mind reader."

"Listen... I'm in love with your father," Ember blurted, the announcement coming out of left field.

Alyssa dropped the dress she'd been holding up against herself in the mirror. She'd wondered when Ember would get around to admitting it. Not that she wanted details about them because... just no thanks. "I know."

"I know this sounds crazy and if you're... wait, what?"

"I've known for a while. I'm pretty sure he's into you too." Given his mood swings lately, she figured he was just fighting the urge to mate. Which was something she really didn't want to think about.

"Do you hate me?"

"No! Why would you think that?"

"Uh, because he's your dad." For the first time ever, Ember sounded unsure of herself.

"So? I want him to be happy. Hell, I want *you* to be happy. You guys are both adults and he's been freaking surly since you moved back. Put everyone out of their misery and go for it." It *was* a little weird, but not enough to bother Alyssa. She figured it might be harder to deal with if they were human, but she loved her packmate and her father and if their wolf side was happy then it was meant to be.

Ember pushed out a ragged sigh. "I expected you to be mad or grossed out or something. Now I don't know what to say."

"Just promise you'll never, *ever*, give me any bedroom details. That's the one thing I ask for. Oh, and I'm not calling you mom. Ever." Alyssa's dad had been lonely, even if he would never admit it. And Ember was not only a good person, she was strong. Definitely the kind of mate he needed.

Ember let out a loud bark of laughter. "Deal. So when are you seeing Reece again?"

"He's picking me up soon and I still don't know what to wear."

"Red sweater, jeans and knee-high boots," Ember said without pause.

"The wraparound one?" She'd been thinking something more subtle.

"Oh yeah. It shows off your cleavage and it's easy access for him."

"God, you really are a perv."

"Uh, yeah. And now I'm going to go sneak into Kayne's house and wait for him—naked in his bed."

"Oh my God! No, no, no." She definitely needed to un-hear that.

"Only time I do that, I swear. Have fun tonight and be bad." Laughing, Ember disconnected.

Smiling to herself, Alyssa tossed her cell onto Charlie's guest bed and tugged the clothes Ember had suggested out of her suitcase. Anticipation hummed through her as she thought about the upcoming night with Reece. She knew they'd be crossing a line and while she was nervous, she couldn't wait to experience everything. Finally.

No chaperones or packmates getting in her way.

***

"I want it official. No matter what happens between me and Alyssa, our packs have a pact of solidarity from any outside threats." Reece's voice was heated and earnest.

Kayne rubbed a hand over the back of his neck, exhausted from the last week and a half. He hadn't talked to or seen Ember since that day in his kitchen and he was feeling edgy. Restless. "Unless you do something to impede on my territory or hurt my pack, that's always been our unofficial pact anyway."

"I know, but I need everyone to know it. Officially."

"*You* need it?" Sighing, he shut his front door behind him. Today had been the day from hell. He hadn't realized just how much Alyssa did for the pack, for *him*, until she wasn't here anymore. When, because at this point he knew it wasn't an "if", she mated with Reece, he'd have to find someone else to handle all the finances and other stuff she seemed to magically take care of. He never should have taken her for granted, or hell, worried that she needed someone to take care of her. She took care of all of them and he'd been too blind to see it.

"Yes. I need it because it will make Alyssa happy. She needs to hear and *know* that our mating—if she'll have me—isn't about our packs. It's one thing for me to say it but if you spread the word that we've drawn up a blood pact before Alyssa and I mate then it proves to her that my choice is only about her."

The other alpha's words took away some of Kayne's tension. This was the way a mate was supposed to act and the type of male his daughter deserved. "Deal. But fair warning, you hurt my daughter, pact or not, I'll gut you."

"I'll gut myself if I ever hurt her."

A smile tugged at Kayne's lips as he made his way to his kitchen. He needed a cold brew and some down time. After being surrounded by packmates since sunup, he was done. "Deal then. I'll let my second-in-command know tonight that the pact is official. The blood signings will just be a formality when you return home."

"I'll tell my second the same."

"Good. When are you bringing my baby girl home, anyway?" Alyssa had finally called him and he'd apologized but he still missed his daughter. The only time she'd ever been away had been at college. He hadn't liked it then and he didn't like it now.

"Soon."

That answer would have to do, he thought, grabbing a beer from the fridge. It popped open with a hiss, cool air rolling out the top. He inhaled, savoring the crisp scent. "Good enough. Keep her safe."

"Always."

As he hung up, the slightest sound from upstairs made him pause. His house was always open to packmates but no one should be here and definitely not upstairs. He'd been in various meetings all day, dealing with one crisis after another when all he'd wanted to do was hunt Ember down and tell her that time was up. It was time for her to make a decision. A week and a few days was more than enough time for her to figure out what she wanted with him.

After setting his beer on the counter, he slipped off his shoes and hurried up the stairs, going into full predator mode. He froze outside the door when he scented Ember. Her scent was wild and reminded him of blackcurrant. But there was something that underlined it, something that was all her.

When his mate died in childbirth he'd been devastated, blindsided. He'd never thought he'd want to mate again but Ember had knocked him on his ass. Outspoken, smart and beautiful, he remembered the first time she'd told him to pull the stick out of his ass when he'd overreacted to something a packmate had done.

He'd never reprimanded her because she'd been right, and he just hadn't wanted to cause her any embarrassment in front of other packmates. His wolf had known she wasn't challenging him for dominance and had been very, *very* interested in getting to know her on the most basic level, so even his animal side had been in agreement in letting the comment slide.

She'd seemed just as surprised as everyone when he'd laughed off her smart ass remark. That was when he'd realized she'd been pushing him intentionally. From that point on their relationship had been defined by her pushing and him letting her.

Until now.

He was taking everything and not letting go.

"If you don't get your ass in here, I'm starting without you," her voice called through the door, immediately loosening the tension in his chest he hadn't realized he'd been holding onto.

When he opened the door and found her splayed out on his bed, completely naked, all coherent thought fled his mind. He was about to claim his woman.

CHAPTER SEVEN

"Is this one of Grant's places?" Alyssa asked as a hostess led them to a seat by the window overlooking the Gulf.

Reece snorted. "No. I wanted tonight to be just about us without extra ears."

She laughed under her breath as he held out the chair for her. "Yeah, that's probably a good idea." Shifters and other supernatural beings had extra sensitive hearing and sight among other abilities, so eating at a shifter-run restaurant increased the chances of being overheard.

When he sat across from her and pinned her with that dark stare, she resisted the urge to squirm. Everything about him was captivating, right down to the way he kept his hair cropped so close to his head. It just made him look even edgier. She wondered what he'd look like as a wolf. Hair color didn't always dictate what color your fur would be, though it did in her case.

"What are you thinking?" he murmured, not bothering to glance at the menu yet.

"Just wondering what you look like in wolf form." She didn't have to glance around to know that no one could hear them. By an expansive window, the place was mostly empty and there wasn't anyone behind them on either side. She guessed it was because it was mid-week and not tourist season.

He looked surprised by her statement. "You'll just have to go running with me to find out."

Before she could respond a server arrived and took their drink order.

"I'd like to go running with you," she said when they were alone again. Running with a non-pack wolf was a big deal. It implied a certain amount of trust.

"Me too." His gaze went molten now and she didn't have to ask him what he was thinking.

She cleared her throat and picked up her menu. More than anything she wanted to skip dinner and just head back to where he was staying. She'd waited long enough to have sex and was glad Reece would be her first. Hopefully her last. A couple months ago she would have thought it was crazy to even contemplate settling down but being around Reece had changed everything. "My wolf feels so calm around you," she said quietly, just blurting it out.

To her relief, he nodded. "Mine does too. For the most part."

"Well, yeah." She hid a smile, knowing what he meant. Her animal side didn't understand why they were waiting to get naked together, but Reece made her feel safe. She knew at her most primal level that he'd never hurt her. "Is that normal?" She didn't say "for mates" because they hadn't used that word since he'd arrived in Orange Beach, but those two words were implied.

"I think so. My uncle never talked much about his mate and I don't know that many mated shifters."

"Your pack's pretty young, comparatively speaking." Most of his packmates were all under forty and unmated, whereas the Kincaid pack and her own pack had plenty of shifters over a hundred. And most of them were coupled up.

He nodded once. "Once my uncle died, the older members dispersed. They didn't like the thought of me taking over instead of his son. Though none of them were willing to challenge me over it. They wanted an older leader." Reece lifted a shoulder and she could tell he truly wasn't bothered by it.

"Why didn't your cousin become alpha?"

"He didn't want to. I… honestly don't know who would have won in a challenge. He's strong and smart, but he simply didn't want the responsibility of a pack."

That was a big admission for an alpha to make. It meant his cousin was as powerful as him physically. "Do you guys still talk?"

A small smile touched his lips. "Damn near every week. He's busy trotting around the globe doing God knows what right now."

"What about you and your uncle? Were you guys close?" He'd never said much about his relationship with the deceased alpha.

"As much as we could be. He was a hard male. Fair, but old school. My father and he had a falling out before I was born." Reece paused as their server returned with their drinks; wine for her and a beer for him.

After the man took their order and they were alone again she looked back at Reece. "Keep going. Please." She wanted to know everything about this male.

Taking her by surprise, he reached across the white linen cloth tabletop and took her hand, linking his fingers through hers. The skin to skin contact sent a shiver through her, especially since she knew how talented he was with those fingers. "After my parents were killed he took me in, no questions asked. And he never made me feel like he was doing me a favor or that he cared for me less because of my father. To him, blood and family were important and he took that seriously. Some days I don't think he knew what to do with me. I was very... strong willed."

She snickered. "Most alphas are."

His lips curved up as he nodded. "Yeah. My father wasn't an alpha though so I think it took him by surprise. When he figured out I had the makings of one, he started teaching me to fight, to take care of myself right away. I miss him. What about you? Was it hard growing up as a pack princess?"

She rolled her eyes at the term. "I never felt unloved. Sometimes I think my dad tried to overcompensate since it was just him raising me." Well, him and the pack. They all took care of each other. It was the shifter way. "He was just very protective sometimes." That being an understatement.

"Good," Reece grunted.

She lifted her eyebrows. "Good?"

He just nodded.

"So… if we decide to maybe…" She felt weird saying the word mate.

"Mate?" Apparently he had no such issue. His eyes went pure wolf as he watched her.

She cleared her throat. "Yes. If we do, are you going to send bodyguards with me if I want to go shopping?"

"No. I'll just go with you myself."

"That's not what I mean."

"I know. And… I don't know. If there's a threat to the pack, yeah, I'll probably go into crazy lockdown mode and give you… uh, ask you, if you want bodyguards."

"Ask me, huh?"

"Yes."

She'd noticed that while he was alpha, he didn't order her around. Even when he'd been annoyed that she'd been dancing with other males, he didn't get all macho and crazy about it like she knew some alphas could. Which brought up another question. "I heard from Max that you came to the Crescent Moon bar the other night. The night before you came to see me at Charlie's."

His fingers tightened slightly against hers. "I did."

"Why didn't you approach me then?"

He paused, clearly measuring his words. "I didn't want to ambush you. I'd just found out what you'd overheard and you looked like you were having fun. I didn't want to give you another reason to hate me."

Their server approached the table with two plates of steaming food, interrupting their conversation. Though she hated to, she withdrew her hand from his. Immediately her entire body mourned the loss of their connection. Soon enough, she planned to feel what it was like to have his skin on hers though.

"Full disclosure though," he continued. "I waited outside the bar and watched you head back to the condo with Charlie. If you'd left with a male, I don't know that I'd have shown any restraint...I know I wouldn't have." A single pulse of energy rolled off him then, the power he contained undeniable.

She shivered at the dominant note in his voice, liked that he was possessive of her. Because she returned the sentiment. Shifters didn't share when it came to their mate.

CHAPTER EIGHT

"This is a nice place," Alyssa said, energy humming through her as she glanced around the living room of the guest condo Reece was staying at. She was barely seeing anything though. The furniture pieces were just shapes as she stared at Reece in the reflection of the sliding glass door. He'd asked her back to his place after dinner and she'd said yes.

There'd been no pretense that she was coming over for anything other than sex, but now that they were here, she was feeling nervous. Not because she wanted to walk away, but because...*sex*. Reece was one of the most powerful males she'd ever met and she knew he had experience. Likely more than she wanted to think about. She was worried she'd be a disappointment.

"You don't want to talk about the condo," he murmured, moving in behind her. Her back collided with his chest, the heat he emanated all-encompassing as his big hands settled on her hips.

"No, I don't." Taking a deep breath, she decided to just tell him the truth. "I'm a virgin."

He froze, that big body going impossibly still, but he didn't pull away. His fingers tightened on her hips. "Do you want to stop?"

"No way." She turned in his arms and linked her fingers behind his neck. She didn't want to stop or talk about anything. She just wanted to feel.

His mouth was on hers before she could blink. Moaning, she arched into him, feeling as if she could crawl out of her skin as his tongue teased against hers. The worry was still there, pulsing through her, but when he kissed her like this it was hard to focus on anything but the moment.

He growled in a purely possessive way she'd only ever heard mated males make. The sound sent spirals of pleasure to all her nerve endings, knowing it was for her, that she brought out this side of him.

Before she could lose her nerve, she reached down and tugged on the tie to her wraparound sweater. Her friend had been right. Easy access was the way to go. When it loosened, Reece pulled back a fraction, looked down.

His gaze was pure wolf as it tracked down to her now gaping top. The cheery red sweater was open, revealing just the hint of a lacy black bra with a red bow in the middle and the curves of her breasts. He'd seen them before but it didn't matter. He let out a groan. "Everything about you makes me crazy," he murmured, pushing the sweater off her shoulders so that it fell to the floor.

She was barely aware of anything as he bent his head to her covered breasts. She clutched onto his shoulders and it was as if he read her mind. He hoisted her up, letting her wrap her legs around him. He immediately began walking, heading... somewhere. She didn't care where as long as it had a flat surface.

Reece stumbled into the first door along the hallway even as he sucked on one of her covered nipples. The sensation of his warm mouth and wicked tongue through the lacy material made her moan.

Her head fell back right as she found herself flat on her back on cool sheets. Reece pulled away, making her reach for him. But he was fast, stripping off her boots, jeans and everything else until she was naked on his bed.

She didn't have time to feel self-conscious. Light from the nearly full moon streamed in the wide open windows, illuminating the room clearly. He was poised at the edge of the bed, his chest rising and falling as he looked down at her. He was, unfortunately, still dressed, but the hunger on his face was enough to make her burst into flames.

"Your clothes, off too." She could barely get the words out let alone form a coherent sentence.

She wanted that skin to skin contact, had been fantasizing about it since practically the moment they'd met.

Without a word, he started a slow strip, unbuttoning his long-sleeved shirt with a deliberateness that drove her insane.

She propped up on her elbows, watching him intently. When she shifted against the sheets, her breasts pushed up farther, not escaping his heated gaze. His fingers paused once on a middle button, then he finished. She sucked in a breath as he let his shirt fall. Everything about him was pure, raw, masculine power.

Her gaze tracked over the cut lines and striations of his muscles, his eight pack. Shoving up from her position, she went up on her knees and reached for him. She grabbed his waist and before she could tug him to her, he was on her, his huge body covering hers on the bed.

She savored the feel of her hard nipples brushing against his chest as she arched into him. This was what she'd been craving. When she shuddered, groaning into his mouth, he pulled away.

"I want to taste all of you," he murmured, feathering kisses along her jaw.

She ran her fingers over his skull, through his short dark hair as he carved a path down to her neck, then breasts. When he sucked on a nipple, hard, she cried out in pleasure.

"I scent you and I get hard," he continued, cupping her other breast, teasing and rolling her nipple.

She wasn't sure how he could talk right now, but his words had the intended effect on her. Another wave of heat built between her legs. Unfortunately he still had his pants on, but they would remedy that soon enough.

"I wanted to throw you over my shoulder and take you back to my place the moment we met, your scent was that sexy." He looked up the length of her body then, his mouth hovering right over her navel.

Words and emotions caught in her throat. That was the hottest thing anyone had ever said to her. Because he was speaking the truth. She'd fallen for this male so hard. He'd come down to Orange Beach for her and she knew he wanted her, liked her, but he hadn't said anything else about mating. She wondered... no, she wasn't going to worry about that right now.

"I never truly understood the mating call or how primal our ancestors were until that moment." His wolf flashed in his eyes, wild and heated. "For the record, I wouldn't have cared if you hadn't been a virgin, but...I like knowing I'll be your first. Your *last*," he growled possessively before he bent his head and kissed a path straight to the juncture between her thighs.

Still reeling from his words, she cried out the moment his tongue flicked over her clit. She'd stroked herself to orgasm before, and so had he, but this was a new sensation. It was better—the understatement of the century. He growled as she moaned out his name, the vibration of it making her roll her hips against his face.

"Reece," she groaned as his wicked tongue teased and flicked over her sensitive bundle of nerves. It was too much and not enough. She needed...more. She felt almost empty, aching.

As if reading her mind, he slid a finger inside her slick folds, gently stroking her as his tongue continued that beautiful torture she couldn't get enough of.

When he slid another finger inside her, she clawed at the bed. "Reece." His name was apparently all she could manage to say.

Oh so slowly, he began moving his fingers inside her, in and out, with a perfect rhythm. Her inner walls clenched around him tighter and tighter. The faster he started to move, the harder it was for her to catch her breath.

She arched against the bed, the pleasure almost too much. When he sucked on her clit, she lost any semblance of control. Her orgasm punched through her without warning. All her muscles pulled taut as the climax spiraled out of control. It seemed to go on forever, the seemingly never ending wave of pleasure hitting all her nerve endings until she collapsed back against the sheets, her breathing harsh.

Reece made that sexy growling sound she felt all the way to her toes but she couldn't force her eyes to open. Not yet. She just needed to adjust to the pleasure. She couldn't believe she'd ever been worried about having a male—Reece—do that to her. Holy hell, talk about a rush.

Her eyes flew open when she felt Reece's mouth skim over hers. She tasted herself on him, the knowledge of that making her face heat up despite herself. That was when she realized he'd shucked the rest of his clothes.

His erection was thick and long against her stomach as he covered her body with his. Moving on instinct, she reached between them and grasped his hard length. He moaned into her mouth as she stroked him, once, twice, three times.

"You're going to kill me," he murmured, before pulling his hips away from hers just long enough to position himself at her entrance.

Her inner walls tightened, wanting to be completely filled by him. As shifters they didn't worry about diseases so condoms were a non-issue, especially since she wasn't in heat.

Slowly, he pushed inside her, clearly taking his time. There was a slight giving sensation but no pain like she'd worried.

"Alyssa," he groaned as he slid fully to the hilt.

She lost her breath as he stretched and filled her. It was a foreign yet perfect sensation. He paused as his cock pulsed inside her. He stared at her, his breathing harsh. "Are you okay?"

"More than okay." Moving on instinct, she cupped the back of his head as she rolled her hips against his.

Just like that, he ate at her mouth like a man starving, though his thrusts weren't as wild as she thought they could be. They were unsteady and uncontrolled, so unlike the man she'd gotten to know, but he was holding himself back, she was sure.

She didn't want that, not now, not ever. She drew back, nipped at his jaw. "Come inside me," she murmured.

He lost it then, a savage growl tearing from his throat as he slammed into her. She tightened her legs around him, meeting him stroke for stroke as he lost himself inside her. As his heat filled her, another unexpected orgasm shattered through her.

Without thinking, she bit down on his shoulder, needing to mark him, to claim him in the most primitive way. It wasn't the mating mark, but she couldn't seem to control herself as she sank her canines into him.

Before she could think about the loss of control, he did the same to her, biting her shoulder. She lost it, the bite of pleasure-pain too much to bear. "Reece!" His name sounded like a prayer and all she could focus on was the mind-numbing pleasure overriding everything.

The orgasm seemed to go on forever until finally, they both somewhat stilled. His face was buried against her neck, his breathing erratic as he gently nipped and kissed her. She ran her hands up and down his back. His muscles clenched beneath her fingertips.

"That was amazing," she murmured, glad she could find her voice. Though she sounded drowsy and knew she was going to sleep soon. She hadn't thought sex would make her tired.

"I'm not letting you go." His voice was just as drowsy and she wondered if he meant for good or just right now.

She hoped he meant for good, but was too afraid to ask.

"Was that...did I hurt you?" He lifted his head as he asked, but didn't move off her.

His erection was half-hard inside her. "Not even a little bit."

His frown deepened. "I should have been more gentle."

She shook her head. "You were perfect." She was glad he hadn't treated her as if she was made of glass.

"Saying thank you feels wrong, but I'm glad you trusted me enough to be your first." A mix of emotions rolled off him as he kissed her gently, almost reverently before pulling out of her. She wanted to protest, to tell him to stop but couldn't find the words as he slid off the bed.

When he returned with a wet washcloth and started cleaning between her legs, she realized that she hadn't just fallen for the male, she'd jumped right over that edge and there was no coming back.

Reece O'Shea was hers.

* * *

Even though moving was the last thing she wanted to do, Alyssa rolled over at the buzzing sound. Reece's phone vibrated across the night stand, insistent and annoying. Pushing up, she glanced at it, saw Sybil's name on the caller ID.

For a moment, insecurities flared inside her, but she shoved them away. The female was a packmate, of course she'd call her alpha. But... it was barely five in the morning. Frowning, Alyssa flopped back against the bed, glad when it went silent.

Reece was in the shower, the sound of the running water and the thought of his naked body tempting. But she was too sore for more and not ashamed to admit it. Shifters were different than humans in so many ways, but after they'd made love two more times over the course of the night and early morning, she was done for a couple more hours at least.

When Reece's phone rang again, this time Ben, Alyssa got out of bed and picked up Reece's discarded shirt. Slipping into it, she buttoned it up and made her way to the kitchen. She knew she shouldn't be annoyed, but Ben was probably never going to be her favorite person so she figured getting distance from Reece's insistent phone was the best thing right now.

The coffee maker was easy and thankfully Reece was a coffee person too, so she started a full pot for both of them. As it brewed, she inhaled the rich, enticing scent. There was nothing like that first sip of coffee in the morning. Not as good as an orgasm, but it was close. She grabbed a banana, headed to the porch while waiting on her caffeine.

Waves crashed against the shore, steady and soothing. She was going to miss Charlie when she left, but knew it was time to head home soon. She'd already started to miss her pack something fierce. While she had no clue if humans experienced that with their families, it was hard being too far from her pack—even if they did drive her crazy with their overprotectiveness.

At a shuffling sound she turned to find Reece stepping out onto the patio—in wolf form. The male was huge and beautiful, the pulse of his power even stronger in this form. His coat was a rich brown with faint reddish patches streaking through in random places. He approached slowly, his dark eyes steady on hers.

She'd know that gaze anywhere and it touched her that he was coming to her like this in his animal form. Unless she was wrong, she knew what he was doing. Even as she had the thought, he nudged her hands with his nose and shook his head slightly—asking her to pet him.

"You're shameless," she murmured, rubbing his head.

He let out a pleased, growling sound before he bared his neck to her. It was unlikely she could hurt him even now, but the baring of his neck was a huge thing. He was showing her that he could be vulnerable with her, let his guard down. It was more important than anything he could have said to her in an attempt to gain her trust.

She knelt and hugged her arms around his neck, inhaled his scent. He even smelled the same in wolf form, all masculine and earthy. As she embraced him, he underwent the change faster than almost anyone she'd ever seen. It always took her a little time and held a hint of pain during each shift as her bones realigned. But Reece shifted with the grace and fluidity of a true alpha, the sight breathtaking.

"Thank you for showing me your animal form," she murmured when he was crouched in front of her.

Completely naked and the most beautiful man she'd ever seen, he brushed his lips over hers. "I'm ready to head home. Come with me?" The hint of insecurity in his dark eyes sliced through her.

In that moment she realized she never wanted to see him anything but happy. The sight of her sweet alpha becoming insecure had her wolf nudging at her, gently swiping with her claws to make it better. She cupped his cheeks and even though she wasn't sure if he meant for good or just for now, she smiled. "Yes."

She tried to shove down all her insecurities about what would happen when they returned to South Carolina, but it was hard.

CHAPTER NINE

Alyssa unwrapped the towel around her damp hair and hung it up on the rack in Reece's bathroom. This morning they'd been in Orange Beach and now they were in South Carolina. She'd texted her dad to let him know she was back in state but that she wouldn't be heading to Oak Falls until later in the week.

She wasn't certain what the plan was for her living arrangements but she planned to bring it up to Reece tonight. He hadn't been very vocal about that and she'd been too insecure to ask. She couldn't put it off much longer.

After food though. She was starving and couldn't think straight on an empty stomach. Grant had let them use his private plane and Reece had hired a company to drive their vehicles back so their flight had been short and easy—and all they'd done was have sex in the private plane. Now she needed sustenance.

As she finger-combed her hair, she heard the faint sound of raised voices coming from downstairs. Worry punched through her. She knew Reece could take care of himself, but still. Slipping on a robe Reece had bought for her, she cinched it around her waist and hurried downstairs.

The voices grew louder and she scented at least four... maybe five other wolves in addition to Reece. Her feet were silent as she moved toward the living room. In the entryway, she paused to see Reece and Ben—ugh—standing toe-to-toe near the fireplace. Sybil sat on one of the couches looking annoyed, along with three other male wolves she vaguely recognized. One she knew though; Andrew Reid, Reece's second-in-command.

The others nodded politely but he grinned when he saw her. "Congrats on the mating," he murmured, holding out his big arms for a hug. He'd only been in town the first couple days when she'd been in their territory, but it was hard not to like the huge wolf.

He wore a blue plaid flannel shirt rolled up over his massive forearms, jeans, boots and sported a full beard. The man looked like he should be carrying an axe and chopping down trees.

"Thanks." She stepped over to him, accepting his surprisingly gentle embrace. "What's going on?" she asked the room in general as she stepped back, because Reece still hadn't looked in her direction.

She understood why though, it was clear that Ben was challenging him and he wasn't turning away from the male. His alpha side wouldn't let him back down. "Everything's okay," he murmured, his voice tempered.

"My brother's just being a dumbass as usual," Sybil muttered. "And for the record, I'm sorry for his jack-assery."

"I'm not being a dumbass and you deserve better than—"

"Than what?" Sybil shouted, jumping to her feet. "God, you're such a dick you don't even *think* to ask me what I want. Even if Reece wasn't mating someone else, guess what, I *still* wouldn't hook up with him. No offense," she said quickly, looking at Alyssa, "but he's not even my type." Her voice was laced with the type of frustration that made it clear she and her brother had had this argument before but the male just wouldn't listen to her.

Alyssa understood that perfectly, gave her a small smile. And okay, she was relieved that the other female wasn't a threat.

Ben wasn't listening though. "With the blood pact in place, he doesn't have to mate her—"

Reece moved lightning fast, wrapping his hand around Ben's neck and lifting him off the ground in a fluid, deadly move. He slammed him against the stone wall outlining the fireplace. She instinctively winced at the cracking sound.

No one else moved to help the male. This guy had challenged the alpha, in his own home, in front of others. No matter what, even if Reece wanted to let it go, his wolf side would never let him. Alpha's had to be in control at all times. If not the others in the pack would grow restless, question his strength and leadership abilities and fighting would break out. Shifters could be savage.

"Let's get something straight right now," Reece growled at him. "I'm alpha. Period. Alyssa's going to be my mate because I love her. Not because I want to strengthen the packs or any other reason you can come up with in your head. You and I are childhood friends and that's why I'm not throwing you out of my pack right now. But I've never been so tempted. Alyssa's *mine*. You say anything about her, hell, think anything negative about her I'll rip your heart out and feed it to wild coyotes." Reece's voice was savage, more animal than man.

Alyssa was going to go back to the "I love her" confession just as soon as possible, but until then…

She hurried over to Reece's side and touched his forearm. "Let him go."

His muscles flexed underneath her fingertips but he didn't loosen his grip, didn't break eye contact with Ben. "Understand that she's my mate, that nothing will ever change that, and if you fuck with her, I'll end your life. Nod if you understand all that."

Wide-eyed and gasping for breath, Ben nodded.

Only then did Reece drop him. Ben collapsed onto the hearth, sucking in gulps of air as another male strode over and hauled him up unceremoniously.

"I'll take care of him," the male muttered, shaking his head in annoyance.

"Everyone else get out," Reece snarled, angrier than she'd ever seen or heard him. He wouldn't look at her as he pulled her close, wrapping his arm around her shoulders.

Not that she was worried he'd hurt her. Never that.

She didn't look at the others as she heard them hurrying out, just slid into Reece's embrace, wrapping her own arm around his waist and rubbing a soothing hand up and down his chest. She could feel his wolf rippling beneath the surface, his animal wanting free to hunt and make Ben pay for disrespecting her.

"Can we go back to that 'I love you' thing you just said?" she asked, shifting so that she was in front of him, her hands on his waist now.

He looked down at her, his wolf raging in his eyes but when he met her gaze, he blinked and it was just Reece again. "I shouldn't have told you like that." His voice was still raspy but she could see he was calmer now as he pulled her close.

"I… love you too. So much." Saying the words out loud was a little terrifying but she loved him so even if he'd just said that in the heat of the moment she wasn't going to hold back. Not with something like this.

"Thank God." He made a sort of growling relieved sound that made her laugh. "I want you to live here with me. Permanently. If you need time to officially mate that's… not fine, but I'll deal with it. I know you do a lot for your pack but they're just going to have to live without you because you're going to be part of my pack—our pack—now. You belong by my side and I don't want to be alpha if you're not my mate."

She blinked, digesting everything he'd said. "I want to live here too and I want to mate soon. Maybe not tonight, but I—"

His mouth crushed over hers in a brutal, fast claiming that was over way too fast. She sucked in a breath when he pulled back.

"Just needed to do that," he murmured. "You can continue."

She shook her head, trying to clear her thoughts. "I don't even remember what I was saying."

"I think you were going to say you'd be moving in here now. For good."

Her lips curved into a grin as she stepped closer against him, linking her fingers together behind his back. "Oh, is that what I said?" Excitement slid through her at the thought of waking up to him every morning, her earlier fears falling away.

"Yep. And you were also going to get naked in the next sixty seconds. I'm pretty sure that's where this conversation was headed."

Laughing, her heart feeling lighter than it ever had, she hugged him closer. "God, I love you."

"Good because I'm not letting you go." His dark eyes had that possessive glint to them that made her toes curl.

That was fine with her. Now that she'd found her mate, she wasn't letting him go either.

EPILOGUE

Two months later

Alyssa nearly jumped out of her skin when she heard the sound of the front door opening. She shouldn't have been surprised though, not with all the packmates that had been coming in and out all day to steal food before the big Christmas Eve party.

They were shameless. Which was why she, Sybil and Andrew had cooked for an army. Well, she'd mainly baked, the other two had done most of the heavy cooking. That was definitely not her area of expertise.

Reece had told her he had a last minute errand to run before the big party tonight and mostly everyone had cleared out to get ready. Not wanting anyone to see what she'd been looking at, she shoved the pregnancy test into her apron pocket—then smiled when she scented Ember and her dad. It had been a little weirder than she'd expected seeing them together at first, but she was over it now.

Stepping out of the kitchen, she met them in the hallway. "You guys are early!"

Ember, wearing a black T-shirt that said OCD—Obsessive Christmas Disorder—on the front, jeans, boots and fake reindeer ears, made Alyssa burst into laughter as she hurried toward them.

"We brought presents," Ember said, pulling her into a big hug before her dad did the same.

"And alcohol," her dad said. "I've missed you," he murmured, kissing the top of her head.

She didn't remind him that they lived about an hour away and she'd seen him literally a week ago because the truth was, she missed him too. It had been an adjustment moving away from her pack, but being with Reece cancelled out most of her sadness.

Not to mention she'd been so busy taking over a much needed role—party-planner for the O'Shea pack. Stepping into that position had been perfect for her and she was glad she got to do what she loved.

"I've missed you too. Both of you." She looked between the two of them, not surprised to see that Ember was practically glowing. Every time Alyssa talked to her, she was giddy about being mated. "You want to grab your bags from the car or get a drink? Most of the cooking is done, I've just got to get changed for the party."

"Reece said he'd put us up in one of the guest houses," Ember said, her cheeks tinging red.

Alyssa snickered. "That's probably better." They were staying for a few days and she so did not need to hear what the two of them did in their room. That was the only downside to supernatural hearing.

"We've got news," Ember blurted, fear and elation an odd mixture on her beautiful face.

When Alyssa looked at her dad, she saw the same mix. Her gut twisted because she couldn't ever remember seeing her dad afraid. "What's wrong?"

"Nothing's wrong. Well, not wrong, it's just scary and awesome. We're pregnant."

Then suddenly she understood the fear from her father. Her mother had died giving birth to Alyssa, and he had to be afraid for Ember's safety. Ember was probably afraid because she was going to be a new mom.

"That's fantastic news. Congratulations!" She pulled them into a big hug, wrapping her arms around both their waists. They were both taller than her but they stooped to wrap their arms around her.

Well, Alyssa could totally relate to that. She'd taken a dozen pregnancy tests today and they'd all come back positive. Now she just needed to tell Reece. But she'd think about that later. "Do you know when you're due, or is it too soon?" she asked, stepping back.

Before they could answer, Reece stepped in the front door. He shoved a square box about the size of his hand into his jacket pocket as he nodded at Alyssa's dad and Ember. "Hey guys. Glad you made it." As greetings were exchanged, her hand automatically slid to the pregnancy test in her apron pocket.

It was pretty early since she'd just missed her period, but the multiple tests she'd taken couldn't all be wrong. When he stepped away from them, the look in his dark eyes as he automatically reached for her was filled with love and adoration. She couldn't wait until they were alone so she could tell him the good news. "I missed you," she murmured, wrapping her arm around his waist.

"Me too." He kissed the top of her head, the action so natural now. She leaned into his embrace, savoring the feel of him surrounding her.

"Guess who's pregnant?" Ember asked, excitement rolling off her in waves.

Reece's grip tightened, all the muscles in his body pulling taut as he looked down at Alyssa. "You told them first?" Hurt filtered through his words, even though she knew he was trying to hide it.

But how had he even known? "No... I, no! Ember's pregnant. How'd you know I am?"

"You're pregnant too?" Ember went into full on squealing mode as Reece stared down at Alyssa.

"You didn't tell them?"

"No, I haven't told anyone. I was going to wait until we were alone." How the hell had he known?

"I stopped by the house earlier when you were out getting more groceries and found your stash of pregnancy tests." His expression was unreadable. She hated when he went into that alpha mode.

She was vaguely aware of Ember and her dad watching them, but all her focus was on Reece. "I wanted to wait until we had privacy, but... I'm really happy about this." They'd talked about having kids, but more in an abstract way. They'd even used condoms when she'd gone into heat, but clearly they hadn't worked. Now she wondered if it was too soon for their relationship.

His expression softened and he pulled out the box he'd hidden moments before. When he pulled off the lid, she grinned. "A baseball?"

His shoulders lifted in an unapologetic shrug as he pulled her into his arms. "Gotta start early with him."

She snorted. "It could be a girl. So you're happy?"

"Having a kid with the woman I love more than anything? Yeah, I'm happy." His expression was intense as he looked down at her. That was a look she recognized clearly. Even before they'd officially mated, whenever she saw that wicked gleam in his eyes, she knew what was coming.

"I think another congrats is in order," her father said, pulling her into another hug as Reece did the same with Ember. Then the front door opened and more packmates spilled in.

"I'm going to be a father!" Reece shouted, apparently making the decision on when they'd share with everyone an easy one.

"Oh my God, I'm going to be a mom *and* a sister," she said, reality crashing over her as packmate after packmate hugged and congratulated her.

She'd never felt more loved in her entire life. When she looked over at her smiling mate she knew without a doubt that she was the luckiest wolf on the planet. And she was so glad he'd come after her when she'd made the mistake of running in the first place.

Thank you for reading To Catch His Mate. I really hope you enjoyed it. If you don't want to miss any future releases, please feel free to join my newsletter. I only send out a newsletter for new releases or sales news. Find the signup link on my website: http://www.savannahstuartauthor.com

COMPLETE BOOKLIST

Miami Scorcher Series
Unleashed Temptation
Worth the Risk
Power Unleashed
Dangerous Craving
Desire Unleashed

Crescent Moon Series
Taming the Alpha
Claiming His Mate
Tempting His Mate
Saving His Mate
To Catch His Mate

Futuristic Romance
Heated Mating
Claiming Her Warriors
Claimed by the Warrior

Contemporary Erotic Romance
Dangerous Deception
Everything to Lose
Adrianna's Cowboy
Tempting Alibi
Tempting Target
Tempting Trouble

ACKNOWLEDGMENTS

As usual I owe thanks to Kari, Carolyn, Joan and Sarah. Thank you guys for all that you do! I'm also grateful to Jaycee with Sweet 'N Spicy Designs for her design work and always working with me. Last but never least I owe a big thank you to my wonderful readers! Thank you all for reading my books.

ABOUT THE AUTHOR

Savannah Stuart is the pseudonym of *New York Times* and *USA Today* bestselling author Katie Reus. Under this name she writes slightly hotter romance than her mainstream books. Her stories still have a touch of intrigue, suspense, or the paranormal and the one thing she always includes is a happy ending. She lives in the South with her very own real life hero. In addition to writing (and reading of course!) she loves traveling with her husband.

For more information about Savannah's books please visit her website at: www.savannahstuartauthor.com.

Made in the USA
Lexington, KY
05 April 2018